Falling from Ego to Humility

It was a long way to fall, from my ego to my humility, and I didn't fall gracefully. In fact, it damned well hurt and I'm still wincing from the pain of those few months ago. It wasn't a day I could ever have imagined though, a few days ago, someone on TV had suggested the unconscious fear of this day is what kept me fighting for so long ... fighting to climb the ladder, fighting to build my empire and then another empire and another, all to keep the baying wolf of fear away from the largest, thickest, most expensive oak doors that shekels could buy. But what do people on TV know, especially ones wanting more glory than the news they're reporting? This hidden unconscious twaddle is just weirdy, lala New Age claptrap, made up to peddle to the hopeless and gullible. Besides, if anything was hiding, it was doing a damned fine job. My mind's as sharp as a needle and I know exactly what's going on in there all the time — only what I put there.

Anyway, there I was, on the up and up, putting distance between the failures who said I'd never make it and the failure they thought I was who made it ... till now.

Philip J Bradbury

Without stories our lives would be dry, non-fictional decrepitudes; dusty, withered data-existences subject to the changing whims of those who think they know and seldom do. In fact, without fables, there **53** would be no life, for even facts are **Moments** a legend, a tale. For example, **With** inoculations cured some people from **Fables** some diseases so there arose the fable that all inoculations cure all diseases, despite the fact that some maim and kill people. Another fable that masquerades as truth or fact is about fluoride. Alcoa, the largest aluminium manufacturer in the world, was facing a $40 million law suit, in 1939, for polluting the countryside with the most toxic element known to man … fluoride. They "defended" that suit by establishing a scientific institute and, quickly and magically, "discovered that fluoride was good for teeth". Such is our desire to believe in stories, we continue to tell the same old lie, eighty years later. Whether it's about the world being flat, the planets flying round **Philip J Bradbury** the earth, Jesus being a blonde pale-face or global warming, all facts are simply opinions, something to be believed in long after they're proven wrong. Opinions are like bum holes - everyone has one and few are interested in yours. Stories, on the other hand, are more honest than facts. They admit, quite blatantly, that they're a barefaced lie - a moving, humorous or fascinating barefaced lie. However, they're not totally honest for, within every made-up, fictional tale, is an eternal truth that touches our hearts and minds - if they're open to such truths - in ways that facpinions can't, for they're what our hearts remember. I challenge you to recall three salient facts from your least loved school subject, while knowing you'll have no trouble recalling a dozen stories or jokes from the same time. The reality is that we're story-remembering creatures and, true or not, we love to embrace, caress and polish any story that comes our way. There are the stories that arise when our egos (finances and reputations) are pricked and there are stories that arise when our egos move aside. These latter stories are not part of the game of survival but are the fecundity of life, the juice of the heart and a savouring for our taste buds. These are the stories told round the fire on balmy summer nights. Savour and enjoy!

Contents

51 Moments With Fables

If you enjoyed this book enough to buy one for a friend - or yourself, your best friend - just scan this Quick Response (QR) Code with your smart phone and you'll be taken to my website at www.philipjbradbury.com

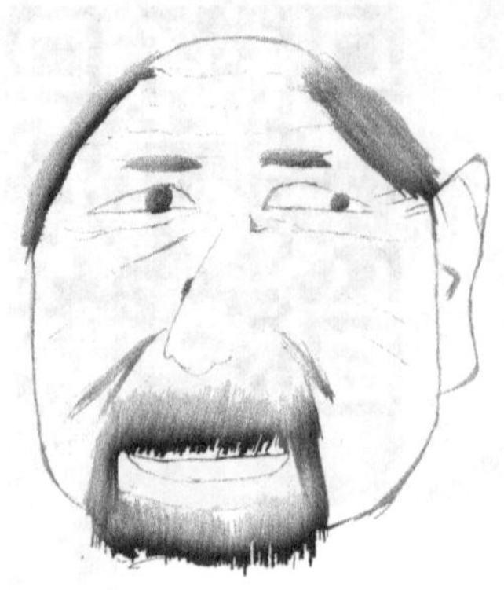

The Birth of Stories

It's 5.00 am, my writing hour, and I write the last story; the story of how the others arrived here.

Along with 520 other trainers, I was made redundant from careers Australia (CA), Australia's largest Registered Training Organisation (RTO). That was April 2016. Along with hundreds of other RTOs, CA had had to face up to the gross dishonesty they had foisted on thousands of naïve students and it was having to repay millions of dollars' worth of fees back to those earnest and hapless students.

Australia's education system is the most ineptly over-regulated one in the world and politicians, with egos larger than their hearts and minds, have all needed to "make a difference". And a difference they've made. Refusing to listen to those at the coal-face – the educators – they foisted the most insanely restrictive system that rewarded the fraudsters and penalised the honest. The way of remedying this has been to enforce more regulations which has had the interesting result of forcing the collapse of thousands of dishonest RTOs and raising a new breed of dishonest RTOs, leaving hundreds of thousands of students out of pocket and partly-completed qualifications, the government deeper in debt and thousands of educators out of work.

After the redundancy I did some part-time work for two RTOs (Australian Technology and Trade College and Australis College) who had me sign their 20-page employment contracts, perform the work and then ignore their own contracts – and Australian law – by refusing to pay me. I did some work for a more honest RTO (Diversity Training) but their honesty and naivety saw them sinking beneath the weight of

bureaucracy and government ineptitude … and the lies of a very slick salesman. They could only pay a fraction of what I was owed and I finally realised my time as a teacher in Australia was over, like so many of my ex-colleagues.It was time to look elsewhere.

I could have gone back to accounting, the career I hated for 20 years and the one that got me into the career I loved for 20 years – teaching. But my heart and soul could not go back and my wife wouldn't allow me to. I became so unhappy and unpleasant when I did what I hated, she preferred starvation to that!

Where else to look?

Aha, the activity I love most – writing. I spent a week travelling round my computer and found 296 short stories. And, in the meantime, I continued to write more. Many were from the once-upon-a-time, distant past and I'd forgotten I'd written them … or remembered them but forgotten what they were about.

I read them and found I still loved reading them – the cynical, the emotional, the humorous, the instructional, the fanciful, the lyrical and the deeply moving. I loved them all.

The sorting task has two sticking points, though.

Firstly, it was not the simple one-of-two-choices type of selection for there was such a variety of tales and types of tales. The task of sorting them into six books was not the task of sorting our rubbish – recycling or not recycling – or the task of sorting our washing into whites or non-whites. It took some time to invent six different categories and, even then, many stories could go into two or more of the artificial categories I'd created.

The second limiting factor was that these tales were my babies. Over 22 years of writing, I'd given birth to these 296 stories – and 20 partly-finished ones, as well as twelve non-fiction books and novels – and I found it emotionally draining to read each one.

There are milestones in our lives and we're brought back to them with the playing of old songs, the hearing of familiar phrases, the wafting of pungent smells, the meeting of old friends and the reading of old stories. I was stilled, time and again, as each narrative rebirthed an old memory, an old regret, an old success, an old failure, an old joy.

But I ploughed on and eventually had six categories:

Fables

Men

Self

God

Writing

Poems/songs

But then, you see, I had run a writing group in Brisbane and currently run two and attend another in Ipswich. These writing groups encourage the spawning of at least a story a week. I had to draw the line and tell the recent stories they must wait for the next train, the next book. I hated to leave some out – it seemed so unfair to them – but books don't become published via the medium of procrastination and soft-heartedness.

So, today's the day – 28th October 2016 – and the books go to press, one by one. Firstly, it's *43 Moments With Men* and, next, it's this one, *53 Moments With Fables*. A random decision, sure, but one has to make black-and-white decisions in a rainbow world.

These are my babies, my children, now grown to adults as I send them out into the world to you and other readers.

I hope they give you as many smiles, tears, sighs, insights and joys as they've given me.

The Lost Story

Once upon a memory a story went in search of a pen to write him down. He searched and searched and searched but all the pens were busy writing down other stories. He didn't know at the time but it was the season for stories, the time of year when stories poured down on the earth. He'd come late in the season but he didn't know that. All he knew was that there was nobody there for him to lay him on the blank, white pages for people to read. He was a small story and knew he wouldn't take much time up for any pen but, still, there were none there for him at this moment and so he floated about – as stories do – feeling sadder and sadder by the day.

Of course, as you know, we can't see or smell or hear or taste or feel floating stories at all. They float round and through us and we never know they're there … well, some people know they're here. Writers are people who can know stories are nearby and when a story comes close enough and knocks on a writer's heart, a secret door in the writer's mind will open and the story will pour through with a huge sigh of relief. However, if a writer is busy with another story, their hearts are busy and their minds are closed and so stories must float on to the next writer's heart to see if it will open the secret door for them to crawl in and speak themselves, through the writer's pen, on to the open and waiting paper.

Our little story's surprise turned to disappointment which turned into dejection. He soon lost the will to search and floated without cause, unsure of what to do next. He hung his head and he imagined what it would be like to give up being a story, to give up altogether, to stop being anything. He didn't know how not to be himself but he tried to imagine it as he hung his head and floated nowhere.

Then a gentle voice boomed through him: "This is your time. Do not give up."

He looked down and couldn't see any humans talking to him. In fact, they were all busily ignoring him and he felt a little sadder.

"This is your time. Feel your strength," said the voice, gentle and strong.

My strength? What strength? He wondered. The voice must be stupid; I have no strength. In fact, he felt quite weak. He looked below him and still no one was talking to him. It must be my stupid mind, playing tricks, he thought and he realised he must be going mad.

"Not mad," boomed the soft voice from nowhere and everywhere. "Not mad, just sad. Feel the strength in your sadness."

He chanced to look up and saw a huge luminous moon rising above the horizon, shining along the rippling, black water. It seemed to be smiling at him. I am going mad, he thought.

"No, not mad, not bad, just sad," said the moon, looking directly at him. Tenderly. Full of care.

"Just sad?" he asked, feeling a trifle silly to be talking to the moon. Only mad people do that.

"Not mad, just sad," said the moon, yet again. "Sad and thoughtful people talk to me and those without a thought call them mad."

"Why do they talk to you then?" The little story asked.

"I am the moon and my light is not my own; it is reflected from the sun. So that's why they talk to me."

The little story did not understand and shook his head.

"I am, you see, the perfect reflector," said the moon, smiling gently. "I reflect you back to you."

"You reflect me …" said the story as a thought passed by, quite closely, and went on by. He wasn't quick enough to grasp it.

"Yes, you nearly got it," said the moon. "Still your saddening heart and let it speak to your mind."

He tried to still his heart thought he wasn't sure how to do that. Another thought floated by and his mind reached for it. It came to him and stayed. It looked like a mirror, a thought mirror, nestled in his mind.

"Well done, you caught it with your still heart," said the moon, clapping … well, it seemed to be clapping but it had no hands … I am going mad, thought the child-story. "I applaud you, young story, you're a quick learner. A mirror in your mind. Think about that."

He thought about it as his heart settled and quietened some more. Another thought floated in and lodged in his mind. He didn't even have to grasp for it this time. It told him something of his mind; that it didn't think anything at all. A non-thinking mind? he wondered.

"Absolutely right," said the moon. "Your mind is like me – a perfect reflector."

"Of what? asked the story, bewilderment hemming him in. "The sun?"

"No, I reflect the sun. Your mind reflects your heart."

"Huh?" asked the story, feeling more hemmed in by bewilderment. "But my heart pumps and my mind thinks; it doesn't reflect."

"Yes, that's what your mind would have you believe," said the moon, its eyes crinkling in a smile. "Your mind wants you to think that it's in charge but it's not."

"It's not?"

"It's not, never has been and never will be in charge," said the moon, rising a little higher in the purple sky. What is true is that your heart thinks and your mind reflects that by getting things to happen around you that prove your heart right."

"My heart thinks? How can it?" asked the little story as more confusion trapped him in.

"Mmm, let me put it this way," said the moon, frowning as he stopped in the sky a moment to explain. "First you feel something in your heart – sad, happy, weak, powerful, lost, clear – and then your mind, busy little thing that it is, makes up a story around you that copies that feeling in your heart."

Yeah, right, keep going …"

"So, you're floating around feeling sad and then your mind, quick as a flash and unable to stop copying anything your heart feels, says, 'Okay, I'll make up a story about sadness so he'll think it's me that's making him sad'," said the moon, patiently. "And so your mind then takes you to all the busy pens and keeps you away from the resting ones."

"Right …"

"So now you think that you're sad because you can't find a pen to take you down," said the moon with a smile so huge it looked like he was saying 'happy birthday' to the story.

"So … so you're saying I was sad because my heart was sad and not because I couldn't find a willing pen?"

"Exactly!" said the moon, clapping its non-existent hands again. "Exactly, young story. You're very clever."

"I don't feel clever," said the story. "I should have known this … but how do I stop feeling sad if I still can't find a willing pen?"

"Firstly, it's nothing to do with pens or no-pens," said the moon, starting to rise in the darkening sky again. "Change your heart, find some happiness in there and see what story your mind makes up for you then."

As the moon said this, the little story's eye was caught by a pen waving at him … well, it seemed to be waving at him over to the left.

"Yes, little story, follow your heart."

The little story turned to the left and floated down into the happily waving pen and he was soon laid out on beautifully clean, crisp, white paper as a story people could read. And now you've just read that little story.

And he's so very happy.

The Golden Belly-Button

Many, many years ago, so long ago, in fact, I forget what this story is about, so I will tell you another. A long, long time ago when I do remember, in the olden days when men were men and so were women, a beautiful baby was born. His parents were so proud and happy, but then they noticed that he had a shining golden belly-button. They were shocked and confused and so were the doctors, but the doctors always were, so that didn't matter. They gave him all sorts of tests and looked in his mouth and under his arm-pits. They were all there (his mouth and armpits) so they decided that everything was in working order and his parents were told to shut-up, that their baby was perfect and the golden belly-button didn't exist.

They did shut-up because they were too embarrassed to tell anyone, but the golden belly-button continued to exist. When the boy was old enough to look down, he saw his golden belly-button and marvelled at the wonderful sight. But his parents made such a fuss about it and wouldn't talk about it, he started to worry. This continued and as he grew, he worried more and more about it and wouldn't let anyone see it. He wouldn't go swimming or sunbathing and bathed under a towel so the light-bulb couldn't see. It got so bad that he would only get changed in the dark so that he couldn't see himself and everyone wondered why he wore different coloured socks and his shirt inside out.

He wanted to get rid of his stupid belly-button and when he was old enough to leave home he went in search of someone who could help him. He went to a belly-button doctor who pondered the problem for a day or three and then rubbed methylated spirits on it to dissolve it.

But that only dribbled down and dissolved his pubic hair and he had a naked willy for two months.

Then he went to a Maori Kaumatua or old man, who said, "When I take out your golden screw, you never have to poo." He thought of the time he would save not having to go to the toilet and that would be great. So the Kaumatua talked to Papatuanuku the Earth Mother, Ranginui the Sky Father and Tangaroa the God of the Sea. Then he put down the phone and boiled up the gall-bladder of a Hapuka fish and the left eye of a Kereru bird. He rubbed the mixture on but the golden belly-button was still there and he had to go to the toilet really bad so that didn't work.

So he went to Australia to see an Aboriginal Kadaiche Man who said he would make him famous. "When I take out your golden screw, everyone gonna say 'How do you do'". He thought it would be good being famous with no golden belly-button. The Kadaiche Man lit a fire and stirred up spinafex sap with a waliru feather, played his digeridoo and said some magic words - "Goo dubba mee awe kutu wanna" which meant "I don' know what to do with dis stupid button, but I hope dis mixture make it go rotten." But the golden belly-button just smiled back and said, "You silly old man, I'm not going nowhere," and that didn't work.

Then he went to America to see a Cherokee Indian Medicine Man whose name was Bent Feather From The One-Eyed Eagle With The Head-Ache Coz A Fast Running Buffalo Stood On Him and he had an extra large cheque-book so his signature would fit. He looked deeply into the golden belly-button, almost drowned and when he had dried himself he lit a fire and burned a cedar smudge and his finger and said "Ouch!" He asked for the eye-sight of the eagle and the strength of the bear and the speed of the cougar but they said, "Not today Man. Don't you know it's our day off." So that didn't work.

He went to many, many other lands and no one could help - the stupid belly-button just sat there smiling and shining. He came to Ireland where he met a Wicca, a wise woman, who said, "So you're the twit with the golden belly-button." And so he left that place.

He was very sad and upset and all he could think of was home and his stupid belly-button. He went back to New Zealand to see his parents but they still wouldn't talk about it. He got very depressed and wanted to shoot himself but he pointed the gun the wrong way and shot

3 chooks. Feeling really sad he went wandering in the bush for 2 days and got lost. He eventually found himself but still didn't know where he was and sat down on a log to cry. After a time he wiped his eyes and realised that a beautiful girl was sitting next to him.

"What is the matter?" she asked.

He told her of all his troubles and this took 61/2 days and he got hungry. When he had finished his story and his stomach stopped rumbling, she said she knew how to get rid of his golden belly-button. She told him that her remedy was unusual but if he believed her, it would work. She was so beautiful and looked so honest and caring he was prepared to believe.

"At the next full moon you must go down to the beach at sunset," she said. "Strip off your clothes and lie on your back on the sand. Do not move till sunrise, and your golden belly-button will be gone."

Then she vanished.

The next full moon he did as she said and lay naked on the beach and waited. He tried to sleep but couldn't so the Sand-Man came down to sprinkle sleep in his eyes, missed and biffed it in his mouth and it took 10 minutes to spit the stupid stuff out. Eventually, he did go to sleep and at midnight a beautiful golden fairy slid down a moon-beam and landed softly on his tummy. She got a golden screw-driver out of her Reebok shoe and unscrewed the golden belly-button. She put the golden belly-button and the golden screw-driver in the Nike bag between her wings and slid silently back up the moon-beam.

At sunrise he awoke and looked down to see that his golden belly-button had gone. He leapt up, full of joy, and his bum fell off.

What's Stuff For, Anyway?

Of course I know that. I'm not stupid. I kinda' know that some people have it a bit hard. Y'know, worse than me coz I see these hungry children in camps and things when I'm switching channels and, like, it's not really nice being bombed and stuff. Maybe I should send them money or something but I don't know where they live or anything and, anyway, I sort of know, like, in my brain, I'm better off than others but it doesn't feel like it. Like, there's sorta' facts and things but, dunno', facts don't make me feel better coz, like saving a panther bear or something that stinked. Well, how's another panther bear or whale in Africa help us all? I ask you; it doesn't, does it.

And, you know, like, all my other friends have ipads and other techinal stuff and all my parents will let me have is this clunky old Samosung and I can't do lots of stuff they do. I mean, it's positively rehisiteric; probably been around way before Pink's last song, way before the stars got invented and stuff.

And they want me to go outside more. I mean, what's outside anyway? Like, we've got six bedrooms and bathrooms and the maid sleeps somewhere and there's daddy's office – all smelly old leather and old fashioned book things – and Mummy has her consternatorium or whatever she calls it, where she has coffee and parties with her friends and the indoor pool and Daddy's twelve vantage cars and, I don't know, lots of other inside stuff so why bother with outside? Just seems excessive to have all this house and not use it.

And then they want me to exercise outside. I mean, what's exercise? What's it for? Like, I don't get running; if they left earlier, they could walk, like, with their friends or, better, go in my boyfriend's car.

And, y'know, I've been thinking about all this consternation and environment stuff. Like, we're running out of things so why don't we save ourselves … save our energy, save our footpaths and lawns and stuff and go by car. I mean, that's using our interrigence, our brains, on the big picture, as Daddy often says.

And they don't like me being inside with my boyfriend and Mummy constantly nags me about boys and doing that thing, 'cept I don't know what that thing is coz she doesn't have a name for it but she keeps going on about that thing and then going red and looking weird and then she shuts up, her finger waving at me.

But, y'know, when I think about it (and I think about it heaps) we're saving on wearing out things outside, even his car – and it's all, like, quiet and not interrupting anyone and we aren't hurting any panther bears or whales or anything and, well, yeah, like, it's really nice and cozy and he likes me so much when we get nearly naked and he gets all twitchy and his hands are nice on me though they shake a bit and he always wants to slide it in and, well, yeah, might be quite nice but I wonder, "What if it isn't nice?" Like, it's not the same as putting on the wrong nail polish coz you can take it off and do it again but if he slides it in and I wish he hadn't, like, afterwards, I can't make it not-happen, him not done me. It's done and can't be undone and so I'm plerplexed coz it feels, like, really good, y'know, down there and I think I get quite wet and his finger smells like it but, like I say, it's not nail polish.

So he gets all twitchy and hopeful and lovey dovey and it's nice but then I just gotta' say stop there and he tells me how much power I have over him but it doesn't feel like power. It just feels like pressure and confusion.

And so I got all these problems and concerns and it feels like I got the hardest life on the world and it makes it hard to concentrate on exstinking species and consternation and hungry babies and other things coz my issues – I think issues is an adult word for adult problems and sounds, like, a bit grand – they get in the way and I can't think of things out there coz they're not, like, in my face like Mummy is and my boyfriend is.

And then there's this nerdy girl, Debby I think her name is, comes up to me all close with her buck teeth and glasses and says I should do some clarity work like, y'know, help some poor people or what 'n I don't know why – maybe just to get her to stop nagging like Mummy – I agreed to help some homeless people. Y'know, get some food and feed them and stuff. So, yeah, I told Mummy I was going to cookery classes – well, it kinda' was wasn't it – and got my boyfriend to drop me off in this, like, back street. Y'know, street lights not all going and rough to walk on in my new spikes. An' my boyfriend was worried and wanted to take me back to my room to do stuff (to calm me down an stuff) but I said I's okay and there's Debbie an' she took me to this old building, all peeling paint and smelly like stink and poor people looking happy and stirring big … I mean, really big … pots of stinky food.

They looked at me a bit funny and an old lady, like, over thirty at least, came over and gave me a filthy apron to put on. Y'know, keep my Vercace skirt clean but the apron dirtied it before anything else did. So I helped get plates and knives and forks out, just like our maid must do, I suppose, and all these dirty, stinking people crept in looking scared and embarrassed and I grabbed a hand and towed it to the food. He smiled but he didn't have teeth – well, not many, anyway – and he tried to hug me but the apron was dirty enough without more dirt on my Fendi top. Others followed and I pulled in the slow ones. Coz, like, if you're hungry, why not eat up. Beats me why they're waiting.

An' I talked to them and they weren't as dumb as they looked. Well, some weren't. Quite interrigent, some of them. And they knew about Ipads and Pink and all the other stars and I, like, didn't expect that!

Debbie thought I should help clean up but I was busy in constervation with some younger ones, like, my age and I went off to see what their homes were like and we didn't have to go far coz it was under a bridge. A bit noisy and a bit stinky but quite comfortable. An' one of the boys started acting like my boyfriend. Y'know, like, all tetchy and close and I looked at a girl – Mona I think her name was – and she nodded and said go ahead, I'd enjoy it and he was really good. Then she slumped down with another boy and so I figured I couldn't regret it if she liked it. I didn't have any power over him and we did it an' it was really nice. A bit messy at the end but it was really nice. He ended up with this strange look on his face, like his eyes were exploding and then he grunted, thanked me and rolled over to sleep.

I wondered if I should have done it but, now, like, I couldn't not-do it, couldn't undo it and then I realised they didn't have their mummys nagging about that thing or their daddys nagging about outside and exercise and they didn't have to go to school and I thought, at last I have some power over me as I looked up at the stars, whoever invented them.

As I realised, before this night, like, until then I knew nothing better. Now I do and I lay down next to the boy, whatever his name was, and didn't even mind when I saw someone sneaking my new spikes. Maybe they'll know something better too and I smiled.

The Gnus

Once upon a time, in the land of Great Creatures, there lived a family of Gnus. Mother Gnu had served up a delicious, hot dinner (badger steaks with prairie grass salad and thistle nuts) and called everyone in to eat. Father Gnu and Little Boy Gnu immediately came in, licking their lips, but Little Girl Gnu was nowhere to be found.

"Oh, no!" said Little Boy Gnu as he rushed from the table, "I bet that Horrible Old Troll has got her. I'll fix him!"

Certain that Little Boy Gnu would handle the Horrible Old Troll, Mother and Father Gnu started eating. However, when no one had come back by the time they had finished their first course, Mother Gnu began to worry that the Horrible Old Troll had got both her children - she decided to see what had happened to them. Confident that his wife could handle the Horrible Old Troll, Father Gnu started on the delicious dessert of deep-fried dragon-flies, candied trout tongue and pureed turtle tails. As he lapped the last luscious lashings of the liquid with his languorous, licking tongue, his limpid, luminous eyes lingered on his wife's lovely, 'luptuous photo, while he wondered if she, too, had been got by the Horrible Old Troll. He lowed lovingly and lumbered leisurely out the door, down to the bridge, where the Horrible Old Troll got him too.

And that, ladies and gentlemen, is the end of the gnus. And now for the weather ...

So, what's the moral of the story? You can choose from:
- The good gnus always end up as bad news,

- Mind your own business, eat your dinner or you'll become someone else's dinner,
- Work together rather than leaving the messy jobs to the little people,
- Maybe horrible old people are actually really nice, when you get to know them, and, when you do, you won't want to go home,
- If you want to buy a gnu's property, employ a troll for your real-estate salesman,
- No gnus is not good news,
- Who cares about the weather when the news is all bad,
- Learn from others' misfortunes,
- Trolls need feeding and/or company too, or
- Who cares?

Take The C Train

If he took the A Train, he couldn't take the B Train. If he left now he couldn't leave later … or earlier. If he wore his black trousers he couldn't wear his camouflage pants. If he stopped to talk to the old lady next door, she might chat too long and he'd miss out on seeing the glamorous girl round the corner … not that he'd ever talked to her but, if she was there, he might get the courage to say something. But he hadn't had the gumption to say anything the last twenty times he'd passed her by so wondered if it'd be different this time. Then, who knows, maybe today'd be different, braver, easier. Maybe she'd smile at him, he'd smile back, she'd say something, he'd reply in his confident, intelligent way and that would be that. Easy peasy! But then, if he waited a bit he'd have more time to think up some compelling conversation … but he might miss her if he waited though he had no idea if she would be there or not.

A hungry lump swelled up in his chest and tried to force itself up his throat. It was too big and he choked as tears welled up and his face sweated hotly. He sat down, swiped his eyes roughly with his fist and tried really hard not to cry, the ultimate proof that he was as useless as he thought he was. He wiped his hands on his black trousers, leaving wet patches and immediately regretted that action. He wondered whether he should change into his camo pants and what would she prefer and realised he had absolutely no idea about her preferences … or anything else about her.

Despite the frantic thoughts screeching round in his brain, there was a deep, dark corner that remained unperturbed by the frenetic insanity round it. He stilled himself – or tried to – and attempted to step through the screeching turmoil and sneak into that still, small space of peace. He managed it for fleeting moments and sighed deeply each time the tranquillity enveloped him.

As he approached and touched the edge of peace again, he heard a whisper:

"The longer you linger, the larger the lion."

He sent a question mark into its depths and it whispered again:

"Tackle the lion when it's a cub and you have a friend for life."

The vagueness frazzled his brain but stilled his heart. Beyond the logic – or lack of it – was an essence, a grain, that settled into his gut with a smiling constancy, dissolving the hungry lump to impotence.

Then, on the greasy slope of habit, he slipped back to the screeching chatter of fear and the sweats started again. With the Herculean effort of someone at the end of his tether, he brought his mind back home to that tiny, safe and peaceful space. His heart slowed, the sweats dried up and a smile crept into his mouth.

Then another whisper:

"We do not fear connection or people. We fear the disconnection from Self."

"Disconnection from which self?" he asked, knowing he has so many selves rattling round in his brain, so many parts that fought with each other.

"The Self of Peace."

"The Self of Peace?"

"The Self that overflows with peace, courage and stillness."

He suddenly knew that Self, the one he'd forgotten to visit while the others fought. Forgotten? Maybe he'd feared, not forgotten, to visit that quiet, graceful Self. It had, he knew, no quarrel with any other, no need for competition, conflict or contempt. It simply swirled in quiet contemplation of its disturbless connection.

Instead of forcing its presence on him, he gave into it, allowing not avowing. It picked him up and, beyond any action on his part, had him striding out the door, up the street and round the corner to see that she wasn't there. He was both disappointed and relieved but had little time for either as his quiet self stirred his legs to strike out for the railway station.

A faint hope withered as he saw she wasn't there either. He wondered if he'd done the wrong thing but was too embarrassed to turn back now – what would the people think of his indecision?

"What do you think of your own indecision?" the voice asked, smiling softly.

He smiled back and realised he'd missed both the A Train and the B Train.

The next train loomed into view, tooting and farting steam while his heart pattered quietly, knowing better than his brain that all was well.

He stepped into the train, heard its departing toot, saw the doors closing and then heard a plaintive "Heeeelp!"

His hand automatically punched out between the closing doors, opening them, and a gasping, florid girl stepped in … the girl of his dreams, he realised. She bore little resemblance to the daunting beauty he'd thought of so often.

"Oh, my God, thanks so much!" she stammered.

"My pleasure, ma'am," he found himself saying, his gallant arm waving her to a seat. He sat beside her, seeing she was less glamorous and far more likeable than he'd previously thought. His mind began panicking, empty of anything useful to say.

"You know …" she said, looking quickly at him and then away.

"Yes?" he asked, uncertainly.

"Aah, um, well, I've seen you go past my place a lot …"

"Mmm," was the only word he could summon and he fervently prayed she'd continue.

"Yeah, well, I always wanted to say something to you but I was too scared."

"Right," he said, his tongue swelling in his throat, stopping further words from getting out.

"Oh, my gosh, I'm so embarrassed now," she said. Looking at the ceiling, her knees, the window … anything but him.

With his mouth out of action, his hand gently landed on hers and she curled her fingers in his while he smiled the smile of a little boy caught stealing cookies. He knew he should say something, real soon, but their combined sighs and smiles were all he needed right now.

The Traveller

A nearly-true travel story

Bigotry takes us the shortest and laziest route to where we want to stay; it allows us to form opinions without the trouble of research. Travel, on the other hand, take us to where we could not imagine being. Opinions bring us security while openness brings us wisdom, sometimes in the most unexpected ways.

It was one of London's steel-grey days; a chilly gloom without shadows and the promise of sleet. The light and warmth of home were an hour away, for most commuters, so we locked ourselves away with floor-staring eyes and politely closed minds, numb to the press of damp coats and twitching mobiles.

I sat while many stood and then, as the doors sullenly opened upon the New Cross dankness, others joined our quietly ruminating herd. There was a reluctant shuffling down the corridor as the new, unwelcome strangers eased their way in; politely apologetic for their intrusion.

A space opened before me and there he was, slumped at my feet. The lurid smell of alcohol and wet wool arose as his crumpled fedora – perhaps once worn with distinction – cringed on the floor.

I suppose I should have leapt aside like my fellow ruminators, lest I be infected by unkempt poverty, but I sat and looked through his black-rimmed glassed to his red-rimmed eyes. We smiled the shy smile of embarrassed strangers who needed not words but acceptance to cover our awkwardness. Though his white beard was an untended hedge, his teeth gleamed white and straight and I suspected there'd been good money spent on their upkeep.

"I'm dreadfully sorry, old chap," he stammered, with an accent straight from the drawing rooms of Mayfair or, perhaps, Downton Abbey.

"No problem, mate," I said, interrupting him, patting his damp shoulder. "Would you like a seat up here, closer to heaven?"

"Closer to heaven," he repeated, chuckling as he surveyed his fellow travellers, all pretending we didn't exist.

"Or are you okay down there?" I asked, picking up his fedora and placing it on his head. I tucked a few unruly hairs behind his ears.

"By Jove," he said, turning to look into my eyes as his smile lit up the room. "Service with a smile." With his elbows over my legs he shuffled his bum and sat up with an erectness that would defy most old people. He brushed his beard briefly and the dust that fell upon his trousers was quickly brushed aside.

"You going far?" I asked, anxious to understand a fastidious man who'd lost his dignity not his spark for life. I was sure his creased face, exaggerating his age, told many a gritty story.

"Going far?" he asked, looking up again. "A mile is too far for a sluggard and a hundred miles is insufficient for the curious."

"You don't want to tell me? I'm stopping in Croydon," I said, hoping my disclosure would encourage his.

"Let us just say that I have nowhere to go and so I'll be travelling forever." He nodded and straightened his trousers, twisted from his shuffling.

"And the traveller is never still, save the presence he calls to mind in every sacred moment," I said, quoting something I'd read that morning.

"Aah, presence," he said, patting my knee, "is the juice of living. Being here in this blessed moment one need neither travel nor change and all the universe arrives in an instant."

"And the stories that have arrived to your presence are legion, I'll bet," I said, dying to open this stubbornly closed clam.

"And stories I'd love to share with a fellow traveller," he said with a sigh. "But I fear my appearance may embarrass and upset …"

"If you're looking for a place to stay the night, you're welcome," I said, apprehensive that I'd startle my prey and lose him to the wind.

"You're not serious …"

"Oh, but I am, mate," I said, my boldness and hope growing.

"But …"

"But nothing," I said, suddenly realising he needed somewhere to stay, to repair and to warm up. And somewhere to feel accepted.

An hour later, he walked into my lounge with a bounce in his step, a shining smile and a gleam in his eye as he surveyed my ill-fitting but clean and warm clothes upon his body. He took the seat I proffered and accepted the plate of steaming stir-fry. He then looked at the ceiling with a sigh on his breath and a tear on his cheek.

Then he began to tell me his story; a story no shunning commuter would ever hear.

Who's In Your Club?

Once upon a time there was a Great White Hunter, in pith hat and safari suit, exploring the jungles of Africa. Ahead of him were his jungle boys, slashing a path with their machetes and, behind were his porters, carrying all his necessary supplies. He had been exploring thus for many months - no white man had ever been so deep into the jungle - when, suddenly, they came upon a clearing. In the middle of this clearing was a massive bull elephant, lying on its side, recently killed. Beside it was a little native man, arms akimbo, one foot on the elephant, obviously proud of his kill.

"My gosh, did you kill this elephant?" asked the Great White Hunter, astonished.

"Yep," said the little native man, smiling hugely.

"But how did you do it?" asked the Great White Hunter, no less astonished.

"With my club," said the little native man.

"Might I see this club?" asked the Great White Hunter, intrigued.

"Oh, there's about twelve of us," said the little native man.

Made in China

Made in ruddy China!" He blurted out, turning the heads of shoppers in the Maroochydore Sunshine Mall, as he waved his beer mat at his mate.

"Hey, keep it down will ya!" whispered Vince, hoarsely, as he furtively looked around.

"But it's ruddy everywhere," said Tommo, his beer mat still swiping at the still humidity of the open-air bar, his voice cutting through the crowd like a band-saw through a frozen chicken – loud and grating. "I mean, what's next. Ayers Rock?"

"Just a sign of the times, mate," said Vince, quietly, sadly. He took a swig of his beer and looked around as if searching for the commotion; as if it wasn't coming from his loud-mouth mate across the table. He swiped some peanuts from the bowl in the centre of the table and chewed.

"Sign of the bloomin' times be damned!" roared Tommo, unable to reduce his volume control. He took a gulp of beer. "Everything's made in China or Hong Kong or India or some other place that's not here. It's just not bloody right," he said, his voice quietening a little as if the build-up of heat was extinguished by the beer he'd just downed. He wiped sweat from his tanned forehead with a calloused hand and wiped it on his shorts. "I need another beer. Want one, mate?"

"Oh, aah, yeah," said Vince, quickly emptying his glass.

Tommo grabbed a handful of peanuts, shoved them in his mouth and weaved between chairs of drinkers, his thongs clacking on the tile floor as he headed for the bar.

"Yes sir, what would you like?" asked the pleasant young man, his white teeth contrasting sharply with his swarthy skin, black beard and black turban.

"Oh hell …" said Tommo, lost for words for a moment, for a change.

"Are you velly okay, sir?" asked the Indian barman.

"Velly what? Ah hell, just give us a couple of beers will ya," said Tommo, quietly, shaking his head.

"And which beer will be your preference, sir?" asked the barman, beaming with gleeful servitude.

"Jeez mate, just a draught, okay."

"A draught beer?" asked the barmen, helpfully, "and would that be a Hahn, Heineken, Peroni or an Erdinger?"

"You got any Australian beers?"

"I'm afraid not, sir," said the barman, hanging his head slightly as would a priest at a funeral. "They seem to prefer the imported ones."

"They?"

"Customers. The younger ones, really."

"Ah, just get me a couple of those," said Tommo, blindly throwing his finger at one of the gleaming beer taps.

"Jeez mate," said Tommo as he got back to Vince, "what beer did you get for us last time?"

"Dunno," said Vince, smiling sheepishly. "I couldn't even pronounce them!" They both laughed and looked around, shaking their heads.

"So what's left of Australia, mate?" asked Tommo.

"Suppose my thongs are," said Vince, uncertainly.

"Ah, excuse me mate," said a woman sitting on her own at the next table. She leant back towards them. "Sorry to interrupt but thongs, or jandals, were invented by a Kiwi shoe manufacturer from Christchurch after he saw the Japanese sandals when he went to the 1940 Olympics there."

"A ruddy Kiwi?" asked Vince, amazed.

"Yeah, mate," said the woman, "Japanese sandals, jandals. That's where the name came from."

"They're from New Zealand from Japan!" said Tommo. "An Australian icon from Japan! What's Australian then?" He couldn't keep his eyes off her. He tried but he couldn't.

"Ya Akubra," said Vince, taking off his hat and reading the label inside. "Nope, sorry, it's made in Hong Kong."

"Hong bloody Kong? You're pulling ma leg!" said Tommo, swinging round like a palm tree in a hurricane. "Chinese buggers make the Australian hat? I feel sick. Maybe I need to get back to the bush."

"But you just got here," said Vince, "on Thursday …"

"Yeah, sorry mate, just joking. Well maybe," said Tommo, quietly now. "I know I said I'd stay for a week. Been a long time since we caught up. But these city places kinda' knock me sideways."

"You sound like me," said the woman at the next table.

"Why don't you join us?" asked Vince. "You're from the bush?" She nodded as she got up.

A sheila from the bush sounds like something I could handle, thought Tommo. Her huge smile lit up the bar and Tommo looked like one of those clowns whose mouths you throw balls into, at the side-show, as they move backwards and forwards. Except Tommo's mouth wasn't moving. His mechanism had jammed and his gawping mouth could have swallowed a sackful of balls.

"Pleased to meet you, ma'am," said Vince as he pulled a chair over for her. "I'm Vince."

"Ma'am? Well, I haven't been called that since Pontius was a Pilot. Thank you Vince," she said, sitting down. "And I'm Sandra." She leaned forward for some peanuts and to give Tommo and good look at her ample cleavage. Well, he presumed it was for his benefit.

"And this one of the seven dwarfs – Gawpy," said Vince, slapping Tommo on the shoulder. Tommo still had trouble unhinging his jammed jaw mechanism.

"He looks hungry. I'll feed him," said Sandra, popping a peanut into Tommo's open mouth.

"Ulp!" said Tommo, suddenly alive as he struggled with the errant peanut. "Sorry Shiela … aah, Sandra, just … aah, shit, sorry aah …"

"What he means is 'Gidday'," suggested Vince.

"Yeah, got that," said Sandra, sitting back with a huge grin.

"His other name is Tommo," said Vince.

"Yeah, look, this is embarrassing," said Tommo, pushing his hat back to scratch his forehead. "So … so, you're just hanging about here? Not much to do?"

"Something like that," said Sandra. "I had time off so thought I'd catch up with a few school friends here. But they seem to have moved on. I also wanted to see the Sunshine Coast and another bit of real Australia."

"And you found it overrun by foreigners," said Tommo with a grin and a sigh.

"Yeah, exactly," said Sandra. "I haven't been here before. Been mainly in the bush. In the Centre and further west."

"Yeah, that's my country," said Tommo. "These beaches are good and all but the heaving crowds of people get my craw. I just wanna' bugger off, go walkabout."

"Huh, you too?" asked Sandra, leaning forward again for Tommo's benefit.

"Sorry Vince, bloody good to catch up but I just get the fidgets in these places," said Tommo, picking up his beer. The beer mat stuck to the bottom of it. He stopped and looked at it like he was about to attack it viciously. Then his grim face cracked into a laugh. "Jeez, you can't even get good beer mats here. The Chinese just want to follow me and me beer to the grave!"

Everyone laughed and downed another quaff of beer.

"Look, guys, I've had a brilliant few days here. Really good," said Sandra wistfully. "But I look around and there's American movies, American computers, Turkish restaurant, Chinese takeaways, Korean cars, Tibetan shops and … I dunno … where's Australia? I can't find it."

"And yer ruddy hat's from Hong bloody Kong!" said Tommo with a grin.

"And I'm not entirely sure where Hong bloody Kong is," she said.

"Just north of Darwin," said Vince, chuckling. "Okay, enough wingeing. Who's for another beer?" Two empty glasses shot forward and he stood to walk off.

"Aw heck, I'm not good at this sorta' thing, Sandra," said Tommo, squirming like he had witchetty grubs in his undies. "I've had a coupla' days down here, Vince, and it's been good. Really good. And I'm staying for a couple more but my feet are itchin' for red dirt and gum tree roots to trip up on …"

"And?" asked Sandra with a huge smile.

"And … you know … you wanna, well …" asked Tommo, dark terror in his eyes.

"I wanna go for a drive, you mean?" she asked. "Go bush for a day?"

"Well, yeah," said Tommo, the dark terror turning to something curious.

"Course I bloody would!" said Sandra, smacking his knee.

"Cripes! Now?" asked Tommo, the curiosity turning to bright, sparkling delights with headlights flashing and horns blaring.

"Yep, now! Let's go!" she said, leaping up. Tommo's headlights blew a fuse and he stumbled out of his chair groggily.

"Sorry Vince, a man's gotta' do what a man's gotta' do," he said as he gathered his wits and started for the sunlit walkway. "We'll be back … dunno … soon."

"We'll keep in contact with our Norwegian phones," said Sandra, grabbing Tommo's arm. Tommo's back straightened like a gentleman and he could have been wearing a top hat, tuxedo and spats, rather than the Akubra, black singlet and R M Williams boots.

"Norwegian?" asked Vince, looking as confused as a goanna in a snake pit.

"This is my ute, the white one," Tommo said, in the car park, about to peel away.

"A gentleman opens the door for a lady," she said, holding his arm firmly.

"He does?"

"He does."

"Can't she do it?"

"Just a custom. You know, looking after your lady."

"Right, okay," he said, opening her door while feeling decidedly awkward and looking around to ensure no one else was watching. No wonder I live on a horse, he thought. No doors to open there.

He went round to his door, stopped and tapped on the roof. "These Holdens aren't even made in Australia any more. Bloody travesty," he said wistfully, more to himself than anyone else.

"Come on, get in. Let's get out of here."

"Oh, yeah, right," he said. Good thing about dogs, he thought, they don't give you orders.

"You know how to get out of here? Where to go?" she asked.

"Nah, not really. Vince did the navigating. But it shouldn't be hard," he said. "Beach over there, sun up there and we just head west." His eyes fell down to see that her shorts had ridden up, tight against her crotch, giving sharp definition … aah, stop that, he thought, get ya eyes on the road. It's just going for a drive, a day out with a Sheila and no funny stuff. Despite the rising heat in his brain, he managed to head off in a reasonably stately manner.

He thought he was pretty good with directions but she had the happy knack of telling him what street to go down, just after they passed it. After a few U-turns they ended up where he'd reckoned they'd be, only fifteen minutes after he'd have been there, going his way. But it's hard to get annoyed with a gorgeous bird who's chirpy, spunky and loves the bush. After an hour or so of driving up and down through the hinterland, he wondered what they should be doing. Do they keep going all day to the space and red dirt he was used to or do they compromise and relax somewhere in the gums. And what were they going to do anyway?

"You wanna' stop somewhere?" she asked, patting his leg. He was sure she could feel the heat rise in his brain again as sweat broke out all over. In fact, he was sure astronauts on the way to Mars could feel it but she seemed unperturbed by it. "Perhaps get out, enjoy the view, breathe the gums …"

"Yeah, why not," he said. "Sounds good." He soon found a patch of gravel beside the narrow road, parked and stopped to look at her. She was looking back at him and he suddenly felt very embarrassed, like a little boy caught stealing his father's beer.

They were beside a stand of gums, the constant chatter of birds and locusts, the endless blue sky and enough air to breathe. He stood there breathing, smelling and smiling. He squashed a mosquito on his arm and felt more at home than he'd felt in a week.

"C'mon dreamy, let's go for a walk," she said. "Stretch our legs."

"Yeah, don't like sitting still much," he said. Unless there's a beer at hand. He went round and she grabbed his hand and skipped off into the trees like a dog on a rabbit's trail. He stumbled after her, wondering what the hurry was. After a ten-minute walk they came to the top of a small hill and she plonked herself down and patted the ground beside her. More orders, he thought. She might be bossy but she sure makes me feel alive. Kinda' bossy and kinda' cute.

She lay back and stared at the sun through the trees as a whip bird snapped its song and rosellas crashed and yelled at each other. He tentatively lay back, thinking that's what he should do, while wishing he'd brought his smokes with him. The perfect place to sit and roll a fag and think of nothing.

She rolled over towards him and looked him dead in the eye. Not quite sure what to do, he lay there till a good idea came up. No ideas arrived.

"Hey, aah … you know … aah, I really like you," she said. She breathed in really deeply as if she was trying to suck in all the air over Australia. "Okay, I'll say it. You wanna' kiss?"

"Kiss? Shit," his mouth said before his brain engaged.

"That's gotta be the most romantic reply I've ever heard!" she said, smiling awkwardly.

"Aah, yeah, sorry …" he said as parts of his brain started to function. Her mouth was suddenly over his and his hand went down her back to her bum.

"Oh, slowly huh," she said, between sucking. God, more orders.

His hand went up her back and she started stroking him through his singlet. Darn, these rules are confusing. Before his next thought she was sitting up, slipping off her singlet and undoing her bra. He sat and stared at a sight he hadn't seen in a long while.

"You want your singlet off?" she asked. A nice order but still an order. As he lay down again, topless, the discomfort of the branch-strewn ground fell away as he focused on her gorgeous body.

"You can touch me if you like," she said as she lay back over him. I'd rather do it without being told, he thought. He was about to touch her when she suddenly wiggled about and her shorts were off. Jeez, who should be taking it slowly?

She saw him looking at the words just above her bikini line and said, "I was conceived while my parents were on holiday." In memory of that event, she'd had herself tattooed: Made in China.

The last known whereabouts of Tomas Magnusdotter was somewhere in Arnhem Land where he was living with a mob of aborigines; so black they were almost blue and as Australia-made as you can get.

Twisting History

We all have discretionary memories, remembering what we want to and conveniently forgetting the rest. The "good old days" always seem to become "gooder" the further away they are, such is the power of our individual discretionary memories.

Our collective memory is endlessly creative. Our written history tells us that Columbus, from Spain, was the first European to land on the shores of America, in 1492. I'm not sure of the benefit of us holding onto this untruth, but we do.

Leif Eriksson (son of Ivan the Red and sometimes called Ivan the Innocent), a Viking from Denmark, arrived at the shores of America in 1001, in a vessel hired from the Norwegian merchant, Bjarni Herjolfsson, with a crew of 25. Leif named the northern part Helluland (Flat Rock Land), the next, Markland (Forest Land) and the third and southernmost, Vinland, (Wine Land). Leif sailed back to Greenland the next spring and his fellow Norsemen took up the challenge. Thorvald reached Vinland but died in a fight with Indians, whom the Norsemen called Skraelings. However, Thorvald's followers spent two years ashore before retracing their journey. About 1006 Thorfinn Karlsefini took people and cattle, meaning to colonise Vinland. Thorfinn's wife bore a son - the first recorded European child to start life in the New World.

Then the Welshman, Prince Madoc, set forth with about 30 men, in 1170, in his 'magic unsinkable ship', *Gwennan Gorn*, which had a lodestone as a compass and horn nails to avoid false compass readings. Willem the Minstrel tells of Madoc discovering a 'treacherous garden in the sea' - the great weedy tract now called the Sargasso Sea. A Welsh clergyman, travelling overland from Carolina to Virginia in 1666, related that he was captured by Welsh-speaking Indians. Later came various reports of Indians claiming Welsh ancestry. Then explorers discovered white-skinned, fair-haired Indians deep inside America. These were the Mandans of the Missouri area and they made Welsh-type coracles and their words for coracle, paddle and many other objects resembled the Welsh equivalents. In 1837 smallpox effectively destroyed the tribe and its traditions were lost.

In 1962 the Russian geographer Samuel Varshavsky suggested that the adventurous Carmelite friar, Nicholas of Lynne, arrived in America soon after 1360. In the late 1970s, study of the old Bristol customs records revealed that ships from this west British port may have been secretly fishing off Newfoundland and even trading with the local Indians as early as 1479 - 13 years before Columbus 'discovered' the Bahamas.

Perhaps there was someone there before Leif Eriksson - perhaps we should ask the people who do not write books (the indigenous people) and we should not be surprised if their verbal stories include other races amongst them, before the Spaniards … and even before the Danes.

What would most surprise us is the historians and teachers immediately changing their texts and lessons - our "authorities", people who know things, are the last to align their discretionary memories to revised truth.

Like the Americans, we New Zealanders have a very convenient collective discretionary memory. Our written and taught history tells us that the first European person to set foot on New Zealand's shore was Abel Tasman, from Holland, in 1642. I'm not sure of the benefit of us holding onto this untruth, but we do.

Juan Fernandez, from Spain, arrived at the shores of New Zealand in 1576. Despite the evidence, our scholars persist in embarrassing themselves by refusing to accept this "new" truth, over 400 years later.

According to Josio Toribio Medina's book, El Pilitio Juan Fernandez (The Navigator Juan Fernandez) Fernandez left Concepcion, Chile and arrived at Easter Island in September 1576.

He left there and, according to the 1911 account of Mohu Terei of the Ngati Porou (the Maori tribe which lives on New Zealand's easterly-most point), it was just before full moon that the Maori were out fishing on their usual fishing grounds near East Cape when they sighted the 'Spanish' ship. The Ngati Porou account spoke of their sighting of the Spanish vessel during the nights of Tangaroa (23rd to 26th nights of the moon) on the night called Whatatitiri Papaa. This day was 1st December 1576 and accords with 63 days since leaving Easter Island.

Another English author, Burney, in his chapter entitled Accounts concerning the discovery of the Southern Continent, gives the date of 1576 and says, 'At the time attributed to Fernandez, it was a discovery of utmost importance, but the information known about it is brief and obscure …'

A Historical Dictionary of 1830 contained an article by Vicuna MacKenna which says, 'Stimulated by the success of his discoveries, Fernandez departed from the coast of Chile in 1576, and discovered at approximately 40 degrees west and southwest a coastline with all the appearances of a continent …'

Fernandez then sailed down the east coast and, according to Captain Cook's diary of his third voyage to NZ in 1777, Tairooa (his 'native' guide) told him, "the ship put into the NE coast of Terrawitte, which is now known as Wellington Harbour." While in the harbour, in seven fathoms of water, he left his 24-year-old son in charge of the ship for several hours while he and his three most senior men rowed to the shore in search for food and water. The crew, bitter at not being allowed to leave the ship and at the favouritism afforded Frenandez's son, killed him and threw him overboard. His helmet, sword and other personal belongings have since been found in the Wellington harbour.

Along with the iron helmet, the Wellington museum recorded that '1 telescope case, 1 idol, 1 carved paddle, 1 carved club, 1 short sword and 2 Feejee clubs were found'. These are currently stored in the Wellington museum.

Captain Cook related that Tairooa told him, "long ago the captain of a ship came into Queen Charlotte Sound. During the stay in the sounds, the captain took a Maori woman (the chief's daughter) to be his wife and she gave birth to their son." The Spanish sailors stayed with the Waitaha people at Waikawa village for 111/2 months, before leaving in late November or early December to arrive at Concepcion in Chile, after a record time of 30-40 days, on 7th January 1578. Fernandez was known as "The Wizard of the Pacific".

Captain Cook was quite taken aback when he saw so much complete human desolation inflicted upon the Maoris of the Marlborough Sounds (of which Queen Charlotte Sound is one), brought about by venereal disease - a disease presumably "imported" from Europe.

Soon after Fernandez left New Zealand, the Waitaha people sent potted birds and dried fish as presents to the Ngatimamoe people across the strait, in the Wellington area. The Ngatimamoe then crossed the strait to investigate the source of this wonderful food and they eventually attacked and killed all the Waitaha people, except for a few they kept as slaves - thus the stories of the white people found their way to the Maori people. Thus, also, the stories of the peaceful Waitaha people were able to be obliterated from oral history. Very few of the Waitaha people survive today and most of them live on the remote Chatham Islands. Their prior claim as Tangata Whenua (original people of the land) has been ignored as history is only ever written by the victors.

And so, in America, the Spaniards are acknowledged for a feat they didn't accomplish and, in New Zealand, they are not acknowledged for one they did - it all seems very fair if you don't actually care about the truth.

Dastardly Dashing Panda Bears

Dastardly dashing Panda bears are not so rare, you'll find, if you find yourself in the place they're found. And it's not so very far from where you are right now; but when you're there it seems to be a place so distant from any other place you might fear you won't ever return. But you will.

It's an enchanting place of yellow mountains topped with blue snow and in the plains, you'll see crops of tartan and paisley, from which your pyjamas are designed.

As you sit in the steely-grey grass or the crackling pink sand, you might wonder to yourself, as the tired green sun sinks in the north and the cheeky salmon moon rises to its left, "By Jove, I wonder where all the wild chaps are." And this, my curious friend, as you grow curiouser by the leaping minute, is how you'll begin to think and speak; in a language dastardly dashing panda bears speak.

You've heard the stories of viscous panda attacks as they slash off the arms of triffids, the heads of darleks and bits of hairy chaps. Fearsome are they to behold, so you've heard, as they unsheathe their scimitars and sabres and sweep, with their monstrous biceps glistening in the moonlight, and a whimpering cry is heard from a cowardly meercat herd or a swankering, sneaky sloth.

But fear not if you're neither triffid, darlek nor hairy chap – studious hippos and particularly welcome – or a fluffy beastie. You see, sleek Burmese cats are welcome as chums, ugly British fluffies are not. Wiggling sausage dogs are dined with and bouncing pomeranians are dined on. Dancing camels are banished while snorty hippos and curly-trunk elephants are befriended. So, my trembling friend, tremble no more – if you are devoid of fluffiness in your elbows or palms, you'll be the best of fellows and invited to tea under the purple puce tree any time of day.

Mind, however, if you have no wish to change anything in their pristine land, you'll do spiffingly. You can wander their fields of tartan lamingtons and paisley bear pies, all growing in jolly profusion in their fields irrigated with orange juice and lemonade. Wander all you like. But if you wound a single slithering snail or multi-footed millipede, you'll feel a swishing scimitar for a brief moment and nothing no more at any time, never, nowhere ever again. They quite like their place just as it is and broach no interference.

You may ask about their swirling green sun, their crunchy pink sand or anything else that piques your curiosity as you sip caterpillar tea – fluffy caterpillars, that is – and munch on tartan lamingtons with your little finger appropriately raised just so and they'll expound for hours. You'll be told why grass groans in the morning, why suns wane in the evening and what secrets the moon holds. You may look astounded when your panda host explains that hawks are brown to disguise themselves in herds of rabbits and then gobble them up when said rabbits aren't looking. You may even be skeptical when she explains that the shy moon rises so high to avoid meeting you and I – it's just not good at small talk, big talk and medium talk and so it only comes out at night when you're asleep.

You may listen and question but you must not argue or try to change their minds for that will raise their ire and a chopping blow may end your glorious tea party and lots of other things you have planned, including living a bit longer.

They are good at having you listen and the harder you listen, the more chummy you'll be. If you've been listening particularly strongly, you may then be treated with their special goodie – a paisley bear pie and paw soup. Only picked as the sun and moon are passing each other on the second Tuesday of the week, these bear pies will have you maudlin and munchly mellow and the after-taste of paw soup will linger deliciously on your lips for months.

These picnics under the pining purple puce trees are not short affairs for an entertaining panda does nothing by halves. It may be weeks before it's time for the dishes to be washed by the green naked camels and for the fascinating chatter of your wise and lively panda dies down.

These picnics, salacious and sagacious though they are amid the aroma of the banana-flavoured puce trees, can be interrupted as the alert goes up and is echoed round the yellow and blue mountains like a mosquito with a fog horn. The call will be the sighting of a rare paisley bear and your attentive dashing panda bear will suddenly, with little to-do and no goodbye, dash to his sausage dog steed and bound off through the steely grass and gregarious gladioli and then leap maniacally upon the hapless bear, usually found feeding on a crop of tartan lamingtons, their favourite food. With scimitar flashing, the bear will soon lose its head and be handed over to the butcher birds for dismantling and then to the pied stilts for enclosure in paltry packets of puff pastry to be planted and tended by the emu gardeners. Nurtured on orange juice and green sunlight, these delicacies will be ready for picking and consumption in around three weeks, just in time for the next picnic.

Your dashing dastardly panda bear will return, leap from his sweat-drenched sausage dog steed and carry on the conversation he left an hour ago as if the picnic had never been interrupted.

It's a mystery to us all – us dastardly dashing panda bear chums – that we can be gone for several weeks, in panda land, and our parents never notice. Panda magic, they call it. And, every once in a while, a dashing panda bear, intoxicated with claw soup and the beauty of his own voice, will agree to guide you back home and stay for a while, as long as you continue to listen attentively and agree to keep fluffy beasties – cats and dogs, mainly – away from them. Otherwise there will be panda … monuim.

Gentleman Only, Ladies Forbidden

Non-fiction about sport by a non-sporting writer

Links is the old Scottish word for that thin strip of wasteland between the sea and the pasture, where sailors would find pieces of wood to hit stones around with. The wild Scots were happy with the impromptu nature of their game but the English, tidy little prats that they were, decided to tidy up Scotland, a messy country. They slaughtered and disowned tens of thousands of carefree lads and lassies from their beloved glens and uplands and gave this wild and untidy landscape to tidy English lords and ladies.

In the process, they tidied up the game of Links by moving it from wasteland to productive farmland, slaughtering and disowning thousands of wild and carefree cows and sheep. They also insisted that it was for men only … perhaps women were too untidy. And so a new name was created for this wonderfully tidy activity – golf, standing for Gentlemen Only, Ladies Forbidden.

Though women are now allowed to join in the swinging, the content of the game has changed little in the last 150 years. However, the form has changed considerably from rich gits in funny clothes … actually, no, it hasn't changed a bit!

So, how is it played?

First, we have a ball. No, not a big soft thing like a football but one with inverted acne that's small enough to become easily lost in the long grass … actually, any grass at all! – and hard enough that it will main you should it pass nearby.

Secondly, we have to move this elusive little killer around. No, we don't kick it or throw it – that would be too easy. Golfers insist on hitting the ball with a club but it's not one. You see, instead of a hunky lump of wood, which would make it reasonably easy, if you could find your sneaky wee sucker in the long grass. Hey, why make it easy? Instead, they've chosen to build these long, slender lengths of pipe with a knob on the end.

With your knob-ended stick, you have to whack your tarty ball, innocently resting in the long grass or wherever you last belted it to, into a tiny hole in the ground. They make this easy by mowing large runways of grass to a millimetre of its life so you can always find your ball.

However, since the aim of the game is to hit tiny acne into this tiny hole with less thwacks that everyone else, they also add challenges. So, along these grass runways they plant hundreds of trees and dig acres of lakes and sandpits to make it tricky. They usually add a bend or two just so you can never tell where that stupid hole in the ground is till you trip in it and break your ankle.

The idea of the game is to get much needed exercise and so they added wheels to your bag of clubs and then invented pushchairs so you don't have to walk anywhere. Some places even issue balls with GPS systems in them so you can easily find your balls. Make the balls hard to find and then add GPS to they're easy to find … yes, it was rich gits who created this bizarre game so we shouldn't expect any logic, should we?

The professionals even have other people to pull their wheeled bags around, saving them even more exercise. These bag-pullers are called caddies and it can be a well-paid job. In 2012, the highest paid sportsperson in USA was a New Zealander, Tiger Woods' caddie. Did I mention wealthy gits wearing funny clothes?

So, let's start playing. You belt this little dimply ball half a mile into a hole you can't see as it's on the other side of a twenty-acre forest and the easy bits of the land are festooned with pesky ponds and mini deserts. It's also interrupted by other golfers, going the other way, who could get a bonk on the conk if either of you are less than attentive. You must do this eighteen times. Yes, there's eighteen little holes dotted over the vast crumpled estate and the person who whacks his ball the least number of times is the winner. Golfers tend to roam in packs of four so you just find three chums to compete against, go whack, whack, whack for a few hours of a weekend and then you've got something to talk about – endlessly and boringly – for the rest of the week.

Aside from handicapped snail racing, golf is the slowest sport on the planet but, despite that, millions of lesser-paid no-lifers love to play lots to watch rich gits getting wealthier by smashing little balls around with knobby pipes. After all, there has to be some compensations for not having a life.

And that is why, my friends, the name of the game has changed from Gentlemen Only, Ladies Forbidden to Gathering Others' Limited Funds.

The Power of Silence

My grandparents, Nana and Pop Bayly, ran a dairy farm near Toko, a small town in New Zealand's Taranaki province. My Nana, I discovered many years after her death, was one of those wise and gentle people you called on when you'd run out of answers for your problems – any problem, it seemed.

One day, three members of the Toko Bowling Club, of which Nana was a member, paid Nana a surprise visit. They had an important and secret request of her.

One of the bowling club members was a problem. Elaine (as we'll call her here) was, apparently, the most bitchy and unpleasant person on the planet and she was making life hell for all the club members. She would complain to you about me, to me about you, start nasty gossip about anyone and everyone and constantly complain about everyone and everything. Different club members had tried to talk to her, admonish her, be nice to her and/or get her to leave the club. All of this just made her more determined to stay and her bitchiness escalated. The club members were at their wits end as more and more people were leaving the club because of Elaine. So here they were in Nana's lounge, beseeching her to have a word with Elaine.

But Nana would have none of it. It was not her place, she explained, to tell anyone how to behave. Her three visitors were desperate and not about to be put off. They pleaded and pleaded and pleaded and, eventually and reluctantly, Nana agreed to deal with the situation. However, Nana's terms were that they must say nothing about this meeting and no one was to ever say anything to her or Elaine about this. She would do whatever she was going to do, quietly and without any fuss.

The next week Elaine came to the club and was as nice as pie – she was the most friendly person there, being helpful and positive about everyone and everything.

And what did Nana do? She told no one except my mother, many years later and so I discovered that Nana did absolutely nothing.

Nana, the astute observer of people, knew that others react to us from how we are, not how they are. The committee members, assuming Nana had given Elaine a strong talking-to, felt embarrassed and/or relieved and were now extra-nice to Elaine. And so Elaine felt happier and was extra-nice to others. Her extra-niceness bubbled and flowed round the clubrooms and a nice happiness infected everyone … not just this day but for many years of happy bowling.

All it took was for one person to do nothing and for three to change their minds.

The Hunter is Hunted

It was not a good day for hunting. The sun was bright and the shadows warned the prey of impending death. Far better a grey and cloudy day for a stalker to listen for footfalls, munching jaws and murmuring beasts. Without the warning shadows to scare the already timid game, the silent predator had more chance. No, not a good day for hunting but there had been a whole moon-turn of bad hunting days and hunger drove the hunter out.

Weakened by lack of food, the silent hunter crept upon padded paws without his usual stealth and awareness. His eyes – slightly blurred and less keen than usual – tried to focus on the movements about, on who had marked the ground and the direction of their goings. Slightly wobbly and determined not to rustle grass or break twigs, the cruising hunter knew that every day without food made it more and more difficult for his body to find nourishment.

In spite of the glare of the sunshine casting shadows across his weakened body, he must find food this day. He forced himself to focus, to be steady and to be deeply aware – more deeply than usual – of the tremors through his feet that told of the goings-on around him. There was the constant rumble of a world on the move and, within that, he must discern and seek out the particular tremors that told of food, precious and juicy food. The earthly rumbling was high as was to be expected – creatures moved more when the sun shone.

And so it was that he found it difficult to hear the close noises, the particular sounds of his patch of earth made by his particular prey. Dulled by lack of food and his senses partially blinded by mass migrations to the sun, he struck out with determination and a little trepidation, for the first time. He had always had his skills, fitness and cloud-cover to his advantage. All he had now was luck and it was only desperation that pulled him forward today. It was not the joy of discovery and the chase – with nourishment as the reward – but a blind need for survival that pushed him out to his accustomed patch in an unaccustomed way.

The grass waved in the sunshine and its shadows rippled around before him, confusing his staring eyes. He moved forward, as he must, and the shadows were soon behind him, as well as in front. He started to feel a little trapped within the swirling play of light and shadow. He wondered, as he darted from spot to spot on this island of giddying shadow-plays, if he was the hunter or the hunted. He soon got a taste of being hunted for the first time. Not a nice taste at all. He faltered, almost darting back to the safety of his lair. For the first time, ever, he tasted fear and he shivered, uncertainly and with his instincts failing him.

He forced himself to stop, to listen, to feel, to focus. What had been so natural, so instinctive, had now to be remembered with intense focus and unrelenting concentration.

As he focused all his weakened senses he felt, within the regular earthly tremors, a particular shudder, a growl, that seemed to be growing and moving towards him. It was not the tremor of a familiar prey and so he faltered again, confused. He listened and felt and looked around cautiously. What was this beast, this potential morsel, that moved with such speed and shaking of the ground?

He turned and felt no more as the lawnmower flipped two halves of the black beetle into its gullet.

Fish and Other Wet Things

There is nothing so worth writing about as the Hex-Headed Fringle Fish. However, because it is so fascinatingly different from anything you've ever met before, it's impossible to put its fascinatingness into words. So I won't.

Instead, I'll relate to you the nearly-as-fascinating story of the Blax-Finned Floodle Paddler, a close cousin to the Urble Fish and distant relative to the Oxymoron Fish, the fish you have when you're not having a fish.

I realise that it's only the ox-brained, flat-footed, chinless wonders of our species who don't know about these fascinating fish … yes, the Urble Fish and the Oxymoron Fish, you dolt … but, just in case you were at the back of the queue when brains were being handed out, I'll make it simple and start from the beginning:

Fish swim in water and water is what we drink. Sometimes we drink water with other water-soluble concoctions that make our brains go twerky and we fall over. The various concoctions are all called alcohol but let's not get mixed up between fish and alcohol. Fish in alcohol makes for dead fish and alcohol in fish makes for very drunken water you wish you hadn't drunken. Anyway, back to the basics:

Fish swim in water and you drink water. So, if you're drinking water you have to be careful not to swallow fish as fish do not like that, apparently. They're allergic to death, I'm told. If the fish isn't so tiny as to slip down your throat it can get stuck at your teeth region, your chops, and both of you will be unhappy – neither you nor fish like the taste of one another. Stinky, yucky, belcht to each of you.

Then, if the fish is bigger than that – like big enough for you to slip down its throat – then the happy one is the fish and the unhappy one is you, if you have any sort of aversion to death … lots of people do.

So now you know all about fish in a desultory, generalised and non-brain-straining way. Let's get back to the Blax-Finned Floodle Paddler, a middle sized fish that you can't swallow and it can't swallow you.

Oh, another thing you need to know – and you probably do unless you are a noodle brained, hedge born crudulite – is that fish do not have legs, like you and I, to move them about. Fish swim in water (did I say that before?) and most of them never get to the bottom so legs are useless. The few who do get to the bottom still don't have legs and that's probably because it took them so long to get to the bottom (aeons and aeons) that their legs forgot themselves off … or, to put it in technical terms, their legular usage factor dropped below the standard deviation mean of the hypotenuse of the water refractive index, inducing a crepuscular distortion that meant that the silly sods didn't grow their legs back when they needed them at the bottom. So the legend goes anyway.

So, if you don't have legs – efficacious things to the rest of us – what do you have to move you about? You have sort-of propellory things that flap and squizzle and beat at the water so that, when the water stays still, you don't. And vice versa. We don't know what the fish call them but we call them fins. Fish have fins at their back ends (which is why, in one language, fin means end) and all sorts of different places along their sides, tops and bottoms, depending on the needs and creativity of each particular fish.

The Far Flung Pan

My little six-year-old mind didn't understand what the yelling was about but my eyes could see my father turning red, thumping the dining table and yelling ferociously, belligerently. They could also see my mother's pleading cries, her bowed head, her sad eyes. Stuck in the middle, I forced my body to stay as still as it could. I even tried to stop breathing and probably did for long moments. I tried to pretend I wasn't there so they wouldn't notice and turn on me.

"Oh, John, why can't we just have …" beseeched my mother, till she was interrupted.

"Because I bloody well said so and that's it!" said my father, his voice going quiet and icy as he stormed out. I heard him thumping round in the porch, putting his boots on and then stamping out to the dog kennels. I dared look up for a second and saw him storming off with five dogs trotting behind him, all happy to be out of their kennels; their smiles at odds with my father's thundering scowl.

"It's okay, Philip, you're okay," said Mum, trying to reassure me as she wiped her eyes. I wanted to help her and wanted to run at the same time. I waited. She sat, alternately staring out the window and smiling wanly at me. I didn't move, not wanting to do the wrong thing, whatever that was.

Life, as we know, abhors a vacuum. When gentle, tiny sorrow leaves a room, her wild, bumptious brothers, rage and vengeance crash in to fill the space. After what seemed a lifetime – in my little life – she suddenly looked up, squared her chin and muttered something about getting him back one day.

"Come on, no point moping," she said, standing up. "Let's get the jobs done and we'll have our own fun, shall we."

"Okay," I said, unsure of what fun she meant in this most un-fun moment.

We cleared the table, stacked the dishes, ready to wash them and she suddenly announced that she needed to get outside for some air. I thought there was air in the house but what did I know. We fed the chooks, collected the eggs, watered the vegetable garden, picked peas and carrots and pottered about outside till she decided she'd had enough air. Time to finish the dishes. By now, Dad must have been gone for a couple of hours and I was still uneasy. She seemed to have forgotten the fight but I hadn't and feared he'd return any moment to escalate it. However, I dried the dishes she was washing and put them away.

Then I heard his footsteps.

"Is that Dad?" I asked, ready to run.

"He's early for morning tea but it must be him," she said, looking at me, puzzled. His routine was legend and he seldom varied it.

"Perhaps he wants to say sorry," I ventured, hopefully.

"Sorry?" she demanded. "I'll give him sorry!" By now she was on the last of the dishes; the large roasting pan. She scooped the pan full of cold, dirty, fatty water and stood there, braced. She timed her performance to the split second and waited with the heavy, grease and water-filled pan weighing heavily in her arms. At the precise moment that we imagined he'd be reaching for the door knob, she lunged.

Mum swung the door open and let him have it. The pan slipped and so he got the rancid water and a pan on the head.

"There, that'll serve you right …" she said, training off.

"Well, that's a nice welcome, Mrs Bradbury," said a strange voice. I had to see who it was, looked around and saw Lionel, the local stock agent, standing there with a smile, dripping clothes and a pan at his feet while he rubbed his sore head.

At that moment Dad appeared and he stopped and frowned. Then he summed it up and laughed the loudest I'd ever heard him laugh. The other two soon joined in and then I did as relief flooded over me.

As far as I know, that day's argument wasn't resolved. It was simply heaped onto the growing pile of resentments to be used as fuel for next week's argument. However, the story of *The Far Flung Pan* is talked about far and wide and is still whispered to children in dark moments to raise a smile, to warn of the rages of sin and to look before you leap.

Miss Conception

There was a young girl called Melinda - a happy, lively and loving girl. Much of her loving nature came from her mother, Belinda, who loved everyone. Like Melinda, Belinda had many friends who called around. The house was a jolly and happy place, usually filled with Melinda's friends who were mainly girls and Belinda's friends who were mainly men. During the day Melinda's friends would come and play and fill the house with their lively chatter and laughter. Belinda's friends would turn up - usually later in the day - for more fun and laughter. In fact, in the evenings Belinda became so busy with all her friends that she had to start a roster and each friend would ring up and make a time to visit. She would then entertain them in the lounge with a few drinks and then go into the private room for a while. It was a very jolly place and everyone who came and went was very happy.

Melinda loved her mother and was very happy in their jolly house. She liked to help Belinda with the jobs around the house and they talked a lot and discussed everything. Her mother was so loving and was friends with everyone. There were some people that others wouldn't talk to but Belinda talked to everyone - even those who said horrible things to her. She always said to Melinda that there is goodness in everyone, if we look hard enough and carefully enough. And if we look at the good bits and talk to the good bits, then they grow bigger and the nasty bits slowly shrink away. Melinda thought that this was wonderful and could see so many good bits in everyone that she had more friends than anyone else.

Then, one day, some serious people knocked on the door. They had serious faces and serious clothes - smooth and dark and quite unlike the colourful and fluffy clothes that Melinda and Belinda were used to. They said that they wanted to talk to Belinda in private and Melinda was confused as they weren't taken to the private room. They were taken into the lounge and Melinda wouldn't leave her mother's side as she felt frightened for her.

The serious people wanted Melinda to leave the room but Belinda said that she always discussed everything with her daughter and she should know what it was about. The serious people got more serious, some went red and they whispered amongst themselves. They seemed to be quite scared or nervous or something and didn't know what to do.

Finally one of them, looking especially serious, red and nervous said that they insisted they be able to have a private conversation with Belinda, as the matter was extremely serious.

"If the matter is that serious, then my daughter and best friend should know about it," said Belinda. "Besides, this is also her home and I cannot push her out of it."

"That is why we are here," blurted out Mr Stern. "We don't think your daughter should be in this house."

He probably wasn't supposed to say this as the other serious people looked at him in a very menacing way.

"I mean ... we ... uurr ... just wanted to discuss your daughter's education," he stammered.

"You want my daughter out of the house so you can discuss her education?" Belinda asked, looking confused.

"Aahh, yes ... no ... well ... we are concerned with the conditions here, the people .... ," he said, trying to explain.

"What people?" asked Belinda. "You mean us?"

"No, no ... the other people here," said Mr Stern, pulling at his ear and looking pained.

"But there aren't any other people living here, just Melinda and I," said Belinda, trying to be helpful.

"What we are concerned about are the other people, the ones who come here all the time," said Mrs Bull, trying to wipe something invisible off her lap.

"My friends!" blurted out Melinda. "Aren't they very happy with me?"

"No ... aahh ... yes ... what I mean is ... well ... its not your friends we are concerned with," said Mr Stern, not actually answering the question, again. "It is your friends, Mrs Joy, that we are concerned with."

"Are they unhappy with me?" asked Belinda. "I am sure they would have said so to me."

"No, they are probably happy, very happy," said Mrs Bull with a sneer.

"Then why are you concerned for them if they are happy?" asked Belinda, sinking deeper into confusion.

"We are not concerned for them, we are concerned about them," chimed in Miss Spent, for the first time, grammatically.

"Are they sick or something?" asked Melinda, trying to find a mental light switch.

"No! They are fine! They are happy and healthy and that's the problem!" snorted Mrs Bull. "They shouldn't be!"

"They shouldn't be happy and healthy?" asked Belinda, astonished.

"They can be anything they like! They just shouldn't be here, with this child," said Miss Spent angrily, with her knees clasped firmly together.

"But I like Mum's friends! They are such nice people and they are always giving us things," said Melinda, with concern.

"Listen, young lady. Let me explain," said Master Bates, a middle-aged bachelor, as he sidled up to her, licking his lips. "The things these friends do here are not nice things and we don't think that it is good for you, for your education."

"But I don't go to school here. I go at school," said Melinda, moving away.

There was a moment's silence while the serious people looked at the ceiling, the floor, their hands, their shoes and everything else except other people.

"This is a very delicate matter," said Mrs Bull finally, rubbing her eye and still looking at the floor. "It is very important that there is no confusion and that you know exactly why we are here."

"So why are you here?" asked Belinda, relieved that the confusion was, at last, to be dispelled.

"I thought we had just told you," said Miss Spent severely, shaking her head.

"I'm sorry," said Belinda, "but I don't understand. You seem to be saying that bad things happen here that could affect my daughter's education."

The serious people all nodded together, slight smiles breaking out.

"I think I need a drink - my brain is spinning. Would anyone else like one?" Belinda asked.

"No thank you. We do not drink," said Mr Stern, rather primly.

Belinda looked confused and went into the kitchen to make a cup of tea. There was absolute silence and the serious people looked at the ceiling and floor and other things for the whole time she was away. Melinda watched them with bemused interest and thanked her mother for the glass of lemonade she brought back with her tea.

"Now, what are the bad things my friends do?" asked Belinda, having had no clarity from her cup of tea.

"Well ... you know ... you do them too," stammered Master Bates, smiling sweetly.

"Well, please, what are these things I do?" asked Belinda, sinking back into confusion.

"The things you do with men," said Master Bates, rubbing his leg. As an afterthought, he added, "with their clothes off."

"But the things I do with them cannot be done with their clothes on," answered Belinda, incredulously. "They are the same things I do with women."

"Well!" exclaimed Miss Spent, with her eyes popping. "What do you do when they have their clothes off?"

"I'll be back in a second," said Belinda, leaving the room.

Melinda noticed that Master Bates was licking his lips an awful lot and Miss Spent was rubbing her knees together. The other two looked very flushed and seemed to find the same part of the ceiling very interesting and absorbing.

Belinda returned with three framed certificates and placed them on the floor before the serious ones.

"Mum, can I go and get ready for bed?" asked Melinda, looking very tired.

"Of course, Dear," said Belinda. "I'll be up soon." She looked at the other four. "I am a trained masseur and physiotherapist," she explained patiently. "I am sorry, but I am very slow and have only just realised why you four are here. You are trustees for the high school that Melinda will be starting next year. Is that right?"

The four nodded silently.

"You were concerned that the name of the school would be in danger if the daughter of a parent who did naughty things went to your school?" she said, as a question.

Again, more nodding.

"And what naughty things do you think I do?" she asked.

"Well, we heard .... that .... aahh," said Mrs Bull, uncertainly, "Some people were saying that you were entertaining these people with drink ..."

"And you assumed the drink was alcoholic?" Belinda asked. They went red and looked away. There was a pause.

"Then you were going off in private and doing these nude things," continued Miss Spent, after the pause.

"And?" said Belinda.

"And," repeated Miss Spent. "And we assumed ...."

"You assumed what?" asked Belinda.

"Well, we heard that these visitors gave you things for your services," added Mr Stern

"Yes, I charge for my services, like everybody else. I am a little different from most, though, as I do not charge a fixed fee. People pay me what they think I'm worth or what they can afford. Sometimes they cannot afford it in cash and give me food or clothing or fix my car or whatever," explained Belinda. "I know it sounds a little unusual, but the funny thing is that I seem to get just what I need."

"Uumm," came the mumbled reply from someone.

"I hope you don't mind me asking, but is there still a problem with Melinda going to your school next year?" asked Belinda.

"Oh! No!" exclaimed Mr Stern

"Of course not!" said Miss Spent. "No problem at all."

"Can I ask another silly question, then?" Belinda asked.

"Of course!" said Mrs Bull. "Of course, anything you want to know."

"Well .... this is just theoretical," said Belinda. "But if I was, say, a prostitute, would Melinda still be able to go to your school?"

"Certainly not!" snorted Mrs Bull, looking shocked. "We are a Christian school and we could not allow people with such low morals."

"But Melinda would still be the same child, wouldn't she," said Belinda. "And she's the one going to the school, not me."

"But it's just not right," said Master Bates. "We couldn't have perverts like that around. It wouldn't look very good at all." He looked flushed and didn't seem to know where to put his hands.

"Thank you. I understand now," said Belinda. "It's been very nice of you to come and explain all this to me. You have all been very helpful." There was a knock at the door.

"Looks like my next customer is here, on time, as usual." she said. "My business cards are on the table by the door if you would like one. I am very good at what I do."

They all stood up and followed her to the door. Master Bates lingered a little and took a card while the others weren't looking.

As she opened the door for them she addressed the new visitor, "Looks like we have an educational evening." she said. "First the trustees and now you, Head Master."

"Mr Stern! Mrs Bull!" exclaimed Mr Beat. "I didn't expect to see you here."

"We were ... aahh ... just visiting," stammered Mr Stern. "Just sorting things out for next year. I'm sorry, but we really must go. Thank you Miss Joy."

As he flopped onto the couch, looking rather flushed, Belinda asked Mr Beat if he would like his usual drink.

"Yes please," he said. "Make it a large whisky if you please. Seeing them has rather upset me."

"Don't worry about that. I am sure we won't have any more trouble from them," she said, with a smile. "I will just say good night to Melinda. I'll be back soon."

"Now, would you like just a massage, or would you like your usual extras?" she asked as she came back into the lounge.

The Grandmother

There was a time upon the long ago when the Grandmother could walk through the Gates of Clarity and into the House of Knowledge. In there, in the library, she could pick up a book, any book. But only certain pages and certain words would be shown to her. So she had to be clear of her intention and her purpose and only then would she know which book, which page, which words she had to turn to.

At this time she had to observe certain rules:

Firstly, she had to acknowledge and thank her God, her Source, at all times.

Secondly, she had to accept that the words she was allowed to see, and take away, were the right ones. She was not given the information her seeker wanted. She was given the words her seeker needed.

Thirdly, she had to return the book to exactly where it came from, otherwise her next visit would be very confusing.

Fourthly, she had to treat the house with respect and shut the door when she left. Also, she had to treat the Gate with respect and shut it when she left.

Then she could return safely to the waking world. If these things were not done, then the Word People would not come with her.

These Word People would then be passed on to the seeker, the person wanting the answer to a problem or a thirst for more knowledge. The Word People would, however, only go at the right time and the Grandmother had to accept the timing from them. They were always ready to pass the words on to the seeker, but the seeker was not always ready. When the seeker was ready to accept the words with faith, trust and understanding, they would be passed on. This might be immediately, it might be several days or it might be never, depending on the openness and honesty of the seeker.

The Grandmother would then summon the seeker to the quiet shelter of her abode and they would purify themselves and pray together. This helped to cleanse the channel so the Word People could pass easily and unhindered by human egos. After the passing of the words, the Grandmother would ask the seeker what they thought of the words, the first gut reaction.

If they were accepted with quiet acceptance and a determination for them to be used for the betterment of all, then the Grandmother would know that she had done well. If they were accepted with anger, indifference or objections, the Grandmother had to look to herself, her methods, to see where she erred. This could be a hard time for her as there was no one to help her in the waking world - it was a lonely, inward road to travel, to honestly question her emotions, her ego, her intentions and her purity. There was nothing to tell her if she was ready again to pass on the Word People, except her own inner knowing. She had to learn to fully trust, with humility, her own being.

If the Word People were not accepted, then they would leave the seeker and he or she would feel more uncertain than before the visit. If the seeker was truly intent on self-improvement then they would, like the Grandmother, look inward at their own heart. This was not an easy time but there was no blame on the Grandmother or the seeker if both were honest in their intentions. They could help each other and this could be a time of great learning.

If the seeker was not ready to accept the Word People at all or to see why it was so, then he or she was likely to become more angry or confused and their relationship with others in the clan would suffer. When this happened, the clan would get together and honestly examine its purity of heart - everyone had to bare their thoughts and expose their true feelings on the matter. If something in the clan was found wanting, then it was addressed and corrected, for harmony had to be with the clan. Again, there was no blame on anyone; it was simply a learning.

If the situation appeared to be entirely in the hands of the original seeker and that person would not accept and change, then this was very hard for all, as the seeker could not remain in the clan - he or she would then live alone, at a distance from the clan, and fend for themselves. This caused much sadness and fear for everyone and, thankfully, this did not happen often.

As the Grandmother was the agent of the change she had to take on the weight of the clan's sadness and fear. The clan had to go on and live in harmony so the Grandmother would take that sadness and fear from them, into the wilderness, and would spend whatever time was needed to release that pain - the clan's and hers - and did not return to her abode until her soul was cleansed and her heart was pure again.

The onus of being a Grandmother was very heavy and these times were very hard. However, while it was always hard work maintaining that pure heart and integrity within herself, it was very joyful to be able to pass on the Word People and see the seeker (and the clan) smile and go forward.

To an observer, the Grandmother's job seemed to be the best in the village – she didn't have to do any manual work, she was always wanted by all sorts of people and she commanded great respect. In many ways, the village life revolved around her words and her presence. Though there were many inward satisfactions, it was a hard and lonely road, at times. Everyone wanted to be a Grandmother until the time they were chosen for the job ….

Three Wise Women

With earnestness we set out to improve the world,
forgetting all the while that the world doesn't actually care.

Every once in a while I hear of an individual or group of people who feel inspired, by spirit or their guides, to do some healing on the Earth. Sometimes there is a feeling that they are the "chosen ones" and no one else can perform this miracle – we are never told the consequences if it's not done. When I hear these things, my storyteller mind immediately takes off on a track of its own, creating bizarre and silly stories.

The most recent of these stories is about three wise women who, in a séance, receive information that, on a certain date and time, they are to be at Aorangi (Mt. Cook) to open a power point, which will allow a new and higher wave of energy to enter, thereby increasing the vibrations of Papatuanuku (Mother Earth) in readiness for the New Millennium leap in consciousness and growth. These Three Wise Women (WWIII) are very flattered to be chosen for this task and they tell many people about this important mission. They are very wise women but very ordinary as well, with ordinary life challenges. As they make their preparations for this historic trip, they discover a few things.

Firstly, Betty's daughter told her that the school play in which she is the star, was to have its opening night on the same date WWIII were to be at Aorangi … and there were dresses to be made and rehearsals to transport her to, as well as her full-time job, home-making and her cake-icing group – how was she going to fit all these things in, along with the spiritual cleansing process that was required before the trip?

Then Agnes, with much time on her hands and always fussing over someone else's troubles, began to notice strange spots appear over her body, along with a huge increase in horniness, which wasn't helped by her husband's reluctance to make love to a spotty wife. The fasting and early morning meditations required, as part of the cleansing process (prescribed by her guides), just seemed to give her bad dreams and diarrhoea.

Bertha, the natural leader of the group, was highly organised and sailed through the intervening two months with ease and perfect organisation. She was continually helping Betty organise her life and Agnes her health, while trying to explain that the blue movies Agnes was sneaking home at lunchtime weren't really helping. Bertha encouraged and organised the other two, ensuring that they kept up their spiritual cleansing and that they had all the necessary clothes, money, tickets, candles and other essentials ready for the appointed day of departure. Of course, Betty had a major problem in convincing her boss that she needed time off and he almost threatened to sack her if she went. However, her resolve was strong and he relented. Agnes's husband just couldn't see how he could cope with meals on his own, so she had to cook and prepare frozen dinners to microwave.

As they left, amid shouts of "You don't love me!" from Betty's daughter, "Where's the microwave kept?" from Agnes's husband, and "Leave the videos at home, Agnes," from Bertha, the trio set off in a less-than-spiritual state of mind. The trip to Wellington was uneventful enough but, as they came to the ferry terminal, Bertha just couldn't find her tickets. Every bag was unpacked twice, the car was strip-searched and still no ticket. By this time, the ferry had left and Bertha was forced to buy another ticket. She was not happy and they left six hours later than intended.

As they came into Nelson, Agnes remarked that it would have been better to go via Christchurch and, in that moment, Bertha realised that she had taken a wrong turning somewhere. Not wanting to admit her error, but realising that time was now short, she insisted that they drive through the night, much to the chagrin of Agnes who had thoughts of a delicious gentleman who may be waiting at their motel. The night was dark (as sometimes happens) and the road was wet and, in a sleepy state, Betty (the driver at the time) lost control and drove through a farm gate and stopped the car in the middle of a muddy paddock. The farmer was not pleased to be woken at 4.00 am and charged them more than the ferry tickets to tow them out. Several hours later they were back on the road again – dirty, tired and angry with each other.

They had to wait three hours in Greymouth for the garage to open before they could get directions, a map and some petrol. The spiritual cleansing forbade wheat, meat and sugar and they couldn't find suitable food anywhere. As well as dirty, tired and angry, they were now hungry. The trip to Hokitika was done in angry (not meditative) silence and, by then, they really had to stop. They were absolutely pooped. The backpackers was adequate, some travelling Germans gave them some vegetarian food and they crashed into bed, exhausted. Both Bertha and Agnes had bad dreams and Betty's snoring kept the whole town awake. Then, with a start, Bertha woke up to find that it was 11 am, on the day they were supposed to be at Aorangi. In a panic, she bullied the other two out and into the car, still in their nightwear. As Bertha drove, the other two tried to change into their warmer day clothes in the Volkswagen, with little success. Then, over the pass, they got a puncture and, in half-dressed state, spent an hour in the pouring rain and wind, changing the tyre.

By now they knew that they would never make it by 3.00 pm – the appointed time. What to do? The whole future of the world depended on these three wise, wet, dirty, angry, hungry, tired and half-dressed women. And they had let down the whole planet, their guides and the progress of the universe. They were devastated! And what would be the consequences? With such a realisation of failure and dire consequences, they collapsed under a tree and cried together. And, in that moment, as their tears flowed together and their unity became complete, they felt an absolute peace and love for each other. Nothing else mattered. Indescribable bliss. Then, as their dirty, tear-stained faces smiled at each other, they heard a tremendous explosion which was, they found out later, a volcano from the distant Aorangi. It was 3.00 pm.

In bliss and confusion, they drove back to civilisation and realised that the event had taken place without their ritual and their blessing. How could this be? Were their guides wrong? Had spirit got it all wrong? In the shelter of a bus stop, with a communal sense of confusion, they wept together and held to each other's shaking bodies for warmth, comfort and support. In that second bonding moment, there was a clap of thunder and the sun burst out from behind a cloud, as a policeman came up and asked them if they needed any help. With his help, they were fed, bathed, clothed and provided with beds, with Agnes sharing hers with the policeman.

The world kept turning, the sun kept shining, and people still bought lotto tickets.

With my storytelling mind still racing, I know that this could be the start of my next bestseller but, in this moment, I must ask myself, "Who do we really think we are?" We live on this Papatuanuku, which is a zillion times larger than us, physically, and a grillion times more powerful, spiritually. And here we are rushing around, wanting to save her! Do you think the birth of Jesus would have been delayed if one of the three wise men had got there late, or not at all? The world won't wait for us. If we're late we'll have one experience, and if we're on time we'll have another. What we learn from it is what is important.

Our only mission on this earth is to find out who we really are. We may do this by being involved in homemaking, politics, business, medicine, teaching, talking to rocks or any of a number of fields and experiences. We are not here to save anybody or anything. We are simply here to know who we are. If, in taking a trip to Aorangi, we realise something about ourselves, then that trip is well worthwhile.

The experience of committing thousands of people to the gas chambers (as Hitler did) is only worth it if we learned something from it. The experience of saving thousands of people from the gas chambers (as Schindler did) is only worth it if we learned something from it. The point of Schindler's experience was not to save thousands (in itself) but to learn something from it. As a consequence, both Hitler and Schindler may have inspired many people to act differently but that is not why they did it, on a soul level.

And as you psychically uncork a mountain or heal some other part of the earth, just remember that the earth doesn't actually care – she can take care of herself very well and, with a wiggle of an eyebrow, can catapult you and your city to devastation in seconds. So, go and do your "healings" but, remember, they are not for Papatuanuku – they are for you.

And no, you are not irrelevant – you are making a difference and if you listen to and act on your own (not another's) guidance, you'll make a huge difference. There is a very fine but important distinction here.

Making a huge difference is your destiny but it is not your responsibility. Let's explain it like this: When you buy your food, you are being responsible to yourself, in keeping your body sustained. You buy the food that is right for you. As you buy that food, you'll make the shop, a food distributor, a manufacturer and a producer wealthier. However, you do not choose your food by deciding who to help out and who not to. Helping them is a natural consequence of your being responsible to yourself. Following your guidance, or life purpose, is your responsibility and, as a natural consequence, you'll unwittingly help others. It is not your job to choose who they are and you'll never know half of the people and beings you unwittingly help out.

So, my Earnest Friend, go and heal yourself (in other words, find out who you really are) and don't pretend it's for anyone other than yourself. Papatuanuku will smile, knowing you're listening and acting on your guidance, but if you don't, she'll keep spinning, Ra will keep shining and people will continue to buy their lotto tickets.

Time For The Trees

The sight of the shimmering leaves of the trees was a wonderful sight below me as I approached. The rustling and waving of the leaves was a nice welcome from friends long since seen. I alighted onto an inner branch, caught my breath and admired the white trunks of the poplar family - so proud and straight but looking a little more tired than I remembered.

"Welcome, Mr Kotare," they greet, smiling and bowing their heads in the breeze, in acknowledgement of my presence.

"Thank you, my old friends," I say. "I am so glad you are still here."

"We hope to be always here, but we don't know that now," they say, with a little sadness. "Is Mrs Kotare with you?"

"Yes," I say, "She will be here. It is such a log way between trees that we now take turns at scouting. She is beyond bird-call so I will mind-call her." I did and she answered that she would be with me after she had finished talking to Mr Kotuku and a Kahikitea family.

"How have you been during our apartness?" I ask.

"Very well, thank you," they say, but they can't hide the unease in their tone. Tree people don't actually tell lies but they don't like to burden us bird people with their problems.

"You seem sad and tired," I say, giving them the opportunity to tell of their concern.

"Things are changing and our aloneness is hard to attune to," they say.

The many other old tree friends who were here are now gone - the Kauri family, the Rimus, the Pines, the Willows and so many others.

It was now many wing-beats to the next family, where my partner is and all about us now is a huge swathe of grass, flowing over the horizon and beyond. Just this little family of Poplars in the swamp by the stream broke the flatness.

"We don't get many callers these days, but we are still here," they say, with a sigh. "Riroriro, Kereru and other deep-forest bird people don't call at all now and with the stream lonely of Fish People, your people don't either. We are surprised and delighted to see you."

I smiled but my heart sank. I had a feeling about the stream and now I knew it was true. Another hungry day.

My beautiful partner arrives and stops on a branch opposite me, panting and relieved. After greetings I told her of the stream.

"We are sorry that the stream cannot hold its life any longer," they say. "We tried so hard to keep the water filtered with our roots, but the poisons just became too much for us all."

I sighed, not knowing what to say. Sadness was everywhere and it took more energy away from the body than did the lack of food. Try as we might, it was hard to find something happy to talk about.

"The more we try to talk to the Man People, the more they walk the other way," say the Poplars. They were like the Bee People and don't talk as individuals - the group was one, no matter how far apart they were. "We ask the Grass Grubs to eat the grass to show the Man where the soil is poor and nitrogen-poisoned and so he kills the Grass Grubs. The Stem Weevils eat the corns to show the Man which ones are sulphur poisoned and so he kills the Weevils. We try to show him where the problems are and we try to help but he just poisons us all and makes it harder for everyone, including himself."

"There must be something we can do," says Mrs Kotare, brightly.

We all agree but cannot think of anything.

"We ask the Rabbits to show the Man where he has fertilized the grass too much and the roots are shrivelled, but he just shoots and poisons the Rabbits," say the Poplars, bewildered.

It is hard to know how to talk to this Man so that he will listen and help himself.

"We have asked the Liver Fluke to show the Man which of his Sheep are poisoned by the fertilizer, but he just poisons the Liver Fluke. We have asked the Crows to talk to the Man but he just shoots them." say the Poplars.

"So, how can we talk to this Man so that he will listen?" I ask.

Silence. Sad silence. No one knows how to do this thing.

"He seems to have taken control of our lives and we feel helpless to help him." say the Poplars in sadness, bowing their beautiful heads.

"He seems so powerful, but listens to no one, it seems," I say, wondering at it all.

"Oh, he does have a master," they say. "One he always obeys."

"Oh!" Mrs Kotare and I exclaim in surprise, wondering what this great being could be.

"Yes," say the Poplars, perplexed. "This master is carried on the end of their arms and tells them and what to do all of the time. They are always looking at it for advice."

"This master must be very powerful," I say, in wonder.

"Oh, yes he is," they say. "They look at him and then say in their head or out loud that it is time to do something and then they rush off and do it. Then they look at Him again, say it is time for something else and rush off and do that. This master has them rushing everywhere, doing all sorts of unusual things. And this master seems to organise it so that they have to rush harder and harder, and they always say that they are running out of time."

"And what is this Time?" I ask.

"We don't know," say the Poplars. "Perhaps it is something this little master needs much of."

We are confused and silent.

"What does this master know?" ask Mrs Kotare. "Why is he so powerful?"

"We don't know," they reply. "We have watched and listened and felt and the only answer that comes to us seems strange."

"What have you observed? What is your answer?" Mrs Kotare asks, anxiously.

"We are feeling weakened from the lack of support from other tree friends, flying people, insect people and so many others, so our feeling must also be weakened," they say.

"But you do have some sort of feeling, some sort of answer," I exclaim, wanting to know.

"You will think us silly," they say, after a pause, " but we feel that the master of Man is his own creation."

We all stop and ponder this one. It seems most strange.

"So, he has invented a master he calls Time?" I ask, trying to make it simple for myself.

"Yes, so it seems," they say.

"And what is the nature of this Time? Does it feed him? Does it shelter him? Does it smell nice? Does it make him happy?" I ask.

"It doesn't seem to do any of those things," they say. "It only makes him rush around and say there isn't much left. And yet, it doesn't seem to have any form or substance."

"So, if it isn't anything to start to with, it's no wonder he is running out if it!" says Mrs Kotare, laughing. Such a cheery soul and always seeing the bright side of life. Such a joy to be with. We all laugh. And then wonder.

"So why does this Man invent something that is nothing and does nothing but make him rush and worry?" I ask, puzzled.

"We don't know," they say quietly. "We must be feeling this thing through all wrong. We must be sickening."

"You may be right," I say, confused and concerned for our friends. The Tree people have never been wrong before. We pour as much love into our tree friends as we can and they thank us for the energy. They feel a little better but, like us, still confused.

We all know that Mrs Kotare and I must go on to find food, much as we want to stay to help and understand. Mrs Kotare leaves first this time, to scout for a likely place, and will call me when she stops.

I eventually bid farewell and wonder if our Poplar friends will still be there when we next pass that way again.

Glossary of Maori words:

Kotare	*Kingfisher*
Kotuku	*Grey Heron*
Kahikitea	*A New Zealand tree, sometimes called the white pine*
Riro	*Grey Warbler*
Kereru	*Wood Pigeon*

The Wychwood Badgers Run

*Living in Hailey, Oxfordshire, UK, I was entranced by the quaint
place names so strove to include as many in one poem ...*

It's a Hailey day with a paley sun
Sending softly beams from the greyly sky
On the moundy green and grassy dew
It's a crispy morn for the waking cows
For a Cotswold land and shivering crow
And this is the time, my smiley friends
To breathe again in Witney town
For the badgers creep to their sets to sleep

(You see) creeping down to Poffley End
On a night so still, you can hear the sun
As it sets itself, behind dark hill
It's the time the Wychwood Badgers run
Stay awake, stay alert
Lest they smile through your pane
And scratch your dirt
It's the time for the Wychwood badgers run

In Delly End and North Leigh town
They're gentle folks who softly spokes
They rub their hands and breathe soft plumes
As the mist does rise and robins chirp
At Chilbrook Farm and Burford streets
The moss does sleep on slatey roofs
And cats do stretch with relief at dawn
For the badgers leave and prey no more

51 Moments With Fables

They say at night in whispering tones
Near Charlbury Road and Finstock Lane
The badgers come with eyes aflame
To wake the dead and shake their bones
From the Windrush Inn to the Ramsden Arms
Sneak dark stories with a twilight drink
Into brains that quake as thirsts are quenched
They may be true or may be not; just badgers know

So smile in your gentle fields and kitchen hearths
As the skylark sings the sun to shining
The day in Charlbury town and Rollright Stones
Is soft and cool and safe as pigeon's coo
But don't forget when the day is done
For Kidlington babes and Banbury youths
The shadows lengthen over badger deeds
Chipping Norton, Stow-on-Wold, you could be next

We know not how or when or why
Such stories are sent to steal our smile
Over woodland rise, through trickling stream
Make no mistake, gentle folks who do deny
The badgers truly doly do
Creep upon stone houses, over dry stone walls
Into children's dreams and old folks recalls
You're never safe from the Wychwood Badgers run

Pukeko Cooking

C alled the swamp hen in most countries, it's called the pukeko New Zealand where it has the reputation of having the toughest meat around, rivalling door knobs and car windscreens. There is one recipe that recommends boiling the bird in a large pot with an old boot. After two days, you throw out the pukeko and eat the boot.

These marsh dwellers with their iridescent, bluey/purply plumage, stubborn orange beaks and delicate red legs, walk and forage the muddy places like uncertain ballet dancers, gently placing one toe at a time. They are strangely reluctant to be caught and, in terrain difficult to pass quickly over, enthusiastic pukeko hunters are often seen trudging home covered in mud, swamp weed and squirmy critters as they emit a gloop gloop sound … and empty handed.

However, let us assume that we have, by some weird chance in a million, snagged one of these pukeko chaps we will cook him up, without the boot. The first job, the worst one, is to remove the feathers. Some recommend dunking the bird in hot wax or fat, waiting till it cools, and then simply peeling said pukeko chap. That, however, is a like peeling a rotten potato and waxed chap usually ends up in the rubbish. The method recommended by the rare pukeko eating enthusiasts is to dunk the bird, now dead, in hot water and then pluck. This way, you either get charred hands or you wear rubber gloves so thick you can't even pick up a beer can effectively. However, we will persist, dunk our bird and surround ourselves in a fug reminiscent of old sacks and dead mushrooms for the next hour while we pull, one by one, reluctant feathers from a greyish, leather hide.

With eyes stinging from the putrid smell, hands burned and blistered and an overwhelming feeling of nausea, we'll continue because the end product is worth the pain … we hope.

We might imagine that the flesh is white, like a factory chicken, but this bird is not fed on bleaching chemicals but on mud-encrusted swamp weeds and mud-encrusted squirmy critters and this gives the pukeko chap a nice greyish tinge in colour and, later we'll find, a faint muddish taste. But that comes much later … perhaps.

Just as the Aborigines cook parenti lizards whole, with the body juices retained to help soften the meat, so we do the same with mister pukeko. If we were to strip out the innards and fry the steaks, we'd have nice little baseball bats for toddlers. So we leave the bird whole and pop it into a large pot of already boiling water. The faint grey will, in time, turn a deeper grey but that is proof of cooking meat, not rotting meat. So now we add our fragrant herbs, with the object being to overcome this fragrantly muddy fug. It's not entirely possible but we'll do our best.

First, we toss in a handful of caraway seeds with their nutty, chewy flavour and then a handful of turmeric. The turmeric will turn the faint grey to orange grey and add a saltish taste to the mud. Of course, the pungent onion is vital to help overcome the wafting fug which has, by now, become a danger to children and small animals in the village. A dozen onions and three globes of garlic will help. We're not sure what it will help but it will help something.

Other fragrant herbs and spices can be added but, like the Elizabethan custom of adding more perfume to a smelly, unwashed body, there comes a time when more fragrancy creates more fug. So be careful. However, we could add, gently at first, chopped nuts and coconut to absorb the growing flatulence – no, it's the bird's, not your neighbour's flatulence – and then we can pop in some rice to thicken the broth. Colourful vegetables like beetroot and carrot may be risked to bring the colour back from a deathly pallor – this may work or it may not … it could, in fact, create a deathly pallor with blood stains. Who knows? Give it a try.

Then, turn the element down to medium and leave the bird to simmer while you lock the kitchen door. Then take a two-day retreat, a long way from home, at a health farm to recover from the inhalation if the sphincter-pinching, nose dissolving fug of rotten, wet socks, gently intruded on by a stinging and insolent stab of garlic and onion. Your eyes may stop running after the two days but it's unlikely.

You must now immerse yourself in many oily fragrant massages in a warm and quiet room that reminds one of a Buddhist temple, without the Buddhists. The cedar wood oil will remind you of newly sawn timber in a dry and quiet forest while the rose will bring back memories of a dew-dusted spring garden. Orange and lavender will bring in their quietly astringent scent of clear water and spice-laden cleansing. You can then finish off with Ylang ylang which will take you to a symphony of odours where you smilingly roll in every gently sweet flower that bees and humming birds enjoy.

So, now that some of the memory of mister cooking pukeko is partly expunged by these cleansing and uplifting oils, you take the twelve-hour flight home, bracing yourself as you don the airline's headphones, listening to the persuasive Tony Robbins who gives you strength to return to your simmering and putrid broth.

Knowing that your toil and trouble are always rewarded, you don the overalls, rubber apron and gas mask, and return to village, observe the funerals of neighbours' children passing by and enter where no man has gone before … or will again.

You're now faced with a difficult choice – do you consume the whole delectable mess yourself, denying others the experience, or do you take it as you would a live bomb, and bury it in a far country? If you take the first option they may bury you in a far country.

The choice is yours, my friends and may all uneaten pukeko rest in peace.

Numb Knees, Carfluted Ears and Spare Zs

This morning I leapt out of bed to find my knees were numb. It was just a surprise, not a problem, as they de-numbed themselves within a minute - it just hadn't happened before and felt weird.

Now, numb knees sounds medically poetic and so is sure to become the next pandemic ... Black Plague, Influenza, Bird Flu, Carfluted Ears, Numb Knees. It fits the pattern and I can just see drug company executives wildly leaping up, commanding their advertisers to concoct yet another million-dollar campaign; this time to scare the bejeezers out of us all and have us pouring in to buy their new magic elixir to save us from Carfluted Ears and Numb Knees (consequence horrendous and unproved, as usual), thereby giving them 1,000% return on their advertising investment. They would, of course, have to provide holidays and other goodies to the doctors who would, then, prescribe the new anti-carfluted-ears and anti-numb-knees snake oil to everyone who didn't need it

I mean, just how many sneezing birds did you ever see? The bird flu was an expensive and profitable hoax, as was the meningitis scare. Though the consequences of meningitis are dire, the cure is simple - good old vitamin C.

We used to have "a cold going round". Then we had epidemics. Now they're all pandemics. What will we have next - cerbademics?

And, talking of knees, who was the great irk, the narfled wallop, who put Ks in front of the N-starting words - knuckle, knife, know and so on? Such an ink- and time-wasting exercise.

Thinking about that as carfluted ears and numb knees beset my body, I realised that we use so few Zs that there must be a huge pile of unused ones, lying about somewhere. In the spirit of drug company entrepreneurism, I hereby pronounce that all C-starting words must now start with a Z. I have zollected all the billions of Zs and now have them for sale, for a Zhristian profit. You, as a zonsumer, need to pay me zash in order to zorrectly spell any word zommencing with C. The zonsequences of not using Zs and Cs zorrectly will be a zerbademic of zarfluted ears and numb knees.

"Zor blimey," I hear you zomment, "I must zanter off to the zhemist to stock up on Zs!"

To which I zallously, zheekily and zryptically say, "Zarry on!"

Letting Others Be Clever

Paul carried the weight of the world quite easily, it seemed. He was (and still is) an extremely good accountant and can spot a misposting at fifty paces and solve business problems that others just can't. This is lucky for the rest of us for there are so many errors and so many stupid and incompetent people around, that we desperately need people like Paul.

Paul would never call you incompetent or stupid to your face – he'd just smile a little, get in there and fix the problem. He might complain about you to his mates and wonder aloud why there are so many stupid and incompetent people around. And, in his quiet moments – which were few as he was so busy fixing the problems of a stupid world – he allowed himself to feel the burden of always being the one who has to fix everything. Why can't others get off their butt, see the problems? Why is always him? Questions like that.

Paul strides through life with such confidence and competence, none of us would know what a burden we are to him. In fact, he's just the sort of chap we want to be, breezing through life with an answer for everyone and everything.

There came a day, though, that Paul's burdens became too much and his coping face cracked. What he revealed, as he let out his frustrations, was that he was the eldest in a poor family of four children. His father's drinking and frequent bouts of unemployment meant that Paul, from age five, had to work for cents to keep the family afloat. Also, he had to help his mother with his siblings and household chores while still having to go to school. Having to fix everyone's problems from that early age, with no father to fall back on, Paul became the master of the universe, learning it was he who had to do all the work and fix everything and never learning to ask others for help – there was no help for a five-year-old and that belief stayed with him for 30 years ... till his face broke.

Through the tears of frustration and loss and anger and every other emotion, Paul got to see another possibility. When this 35-year-old man stopped living in his five-year-old world, he realised he could drop the burden of the world where it belonged, in that shabby house of his upbringing. The tears of his pain and anger seemed to cleanse his sight and he soon noticed some very competent and clever people coming into his life – people who could fix things. In fact, some of these clever people had always been there – he just hadn't noticed their competence before.

It was strange to Paul that when he changed his mind about people, they changed – honouring people made them honourable. Of course, he still slips up and fixes things that don't need to be but, most of the time, he enjoys the freedom of seeing others as capable and competent and his face is now permanently cracked ... in a smile.

Train of Thought

A story of the ordinary world that turns supernatural

Feeling superior to be the only passenger enjoying the sun-buttered streets, the shadowing apartments and passing vehicles, I wondered where all the people were. Probably mesmerised by their little masters, their bawling electronic babies that needed tending every waking minute. While everyone else shut themselves off from the beauty of the real world, I had it to myself. I was relieved and smug that I wasn't addicted and shut off from the passing scenery.

But smug quickly turned to shame as I realised we were pulling out of the station I had meant to disembark at. I hid my embarrassment behind a placid face while my mind raced in two opposite directions – backwards to berate myself for being such a dope and to wonder how I'd done it as well as forward to strategise my next move, knowing I'd miss the job interview and the job … by being less attentive than all those addicted to their smart-arse phones, ipads or whatever it was they were peering at.

"You miss your drop-off?" asked the youth beside me, not looking up from his device. His tumble of black curls made it impossible to see whether he was smiling or not.

"Aah, yeah, aah, how did you know?" I asked, bewildered.

"My compuhand just registered embarrassment and annoyance," he said flatly. "You're the closest to it."

Quite obvious, really, I thought, sarcastically. How could he not find comfort in my discomfort? I would have, if the tables were turned.

"So what does it tell you?" I asked, risking his derision about my techno-idiocy.

"It tells me when to get off, what time I'll be home and what time dinner will be ready, for a start," he said, without pride or sarcasm, as if he was reading a grocery list.

They might make you on time but did they make you flat and boring? I wondered.

"How does it know about your dinner?"

"I programmed it before and, therefore, can forget it because it will remind me." He didn't seem annoyed or excited.

"Can it tell you what to do when you mess up and miss an important conversation?" I asked, eager for humour and desperate for answers.

"It could calculate the curvature."

"Curvature?" I asked, wondering what the heck that had to do with mess-ups and late appointments.

"Curvature of the wave."

"Curvature of the wave?" I asked, repeating his words as I couldn't find any of my own.

"The wave of time."

"Right, I'd heard that time moves in waves," I said, my mind clutching at the precipice of understanding with slipping fingers.

"If we increase the curvature of the wave, time folds back on itself if we bring in a negative coefficient. Or, if we bring the coefficient to zero, time stops."

"Stops inside itself," I said, repeating his words again, for the same reason, again.

"Would you like to go back in time or just have it stop while you jump the cattle-stop to where you were to get off this train?"

"Cattle-stop?"

"If time stops when you don't, it gives you choices but it's a rough ride."

"Look, is this for real? Like, are you pulling my leg?" I asked, looking out the train's window at the passing scenery, just to check I hadn't left the planet for some other dimension.

"We do not tell lies," he said with a certainty that I had to believe. I still couldn't see his face beyond the fall of hair so had to trust his words. "Would you like a test drive?" He quickly moved his right hand over something in his left hand as if he already knew my answer. "Here, I've budded a youngling for you. Hold out your left hand. I complied obediently and a sliver of something dark and transparent slid from his left hand to mine. It tingled and settled in my palm, taking up every curve and wrinkle. I looked at it and a small face peered at me.

"Smile back. Make him feel welcome," he said, flatly. I obeyed dumbly, not believing my smile. The thing – did he call it a compuhand? – believed it and smiled back.

"Okay, if this is real – and I'm not sure it is – I'd like to go back to Norman Park station and be there when I was originally planning to be there," I said. The machine … the compuhand … started blinking and the face burst into a huge smile when I said okay, as if it already knew what I was about to say.

It was subtle and quiet, at first. The awareness crept up on me and I realised something had been happening some time after it started … if I can use the word time loosely here.

It was as if the outer world – the shaggy youth, the seats, the train, the scenery – were slipping away from me. As if I was still on my way to Cleveland, away from Norman Park, but they were returning to Norman Park. Then an awareness grew that my own body – along with the other ones, the train and scenery – was slipping back away from me, as if I had become unhinged from the familiar, tangible world.

A deep peace descended; unbidden and a sense of utter clarity enfolded me. Wrapped in a silken, shimmering blanket of freedom, I perceived that all choices were mine and that felt wild and precarious, inspiring and unsettling. I had a choice to feel fear or excitement and fear brought on the cattle-stop, a jangly, juddering pain, and so I chose excitement and all turned to serenity. The passing, familiar world turned from one of longing to one to simply observe.

But I had a mission, an appointment, and it called me in. There was a moment of resistance and the juddering pain arose so I let go and contentment returned.

Without tangible movement or awareness, I was hovering over the Norman Park station, watching an approaching train. It stopped and I stepped off and blithely walked off to my appointment while this other me, this hovering, observing me, merged back into the walking me, excited and slightly apprehensive.

The interview went well and I am now the Queensland sales Director of Compupalms Corporation, quite unable to remove the square red welt on my left palm.

The Silent Caller

Theme: Suddenly, every radio station in the world turns to whiter noise and a voice reads out a single name ...

London's grey and sordid winter's day was still and foreboding. Something was about to happen – we all knew this – but no one knew what it was. Three million commuters were filling their cars, the trains and buses. All routes out of that darkly charming city were jammed. We just knew, somehow, that we should leave early. Be out of there.

Some blamed the impending storm, creeping down from the festering North Sea, some suddenly felt ill. The rest of us just felt ourselves impelled along by some unknown force. Some, who believed, explained it as God's hand gently at their backs, urging them out and home.

I just found my work was done and, instead of my usual creative idleness, pretending to be busy when I'm not, I decided to go home. I put the fear of an intimidating and pernicious boss aside, stood up and saw the office was empty! Unaccustomed to this unsettling tranquillity, I dashed out the door and then dashed back in, realising I'd forgotten my briefcase. I stood at my desk, quivering and pretending to myself (there was no one else to pretend to) I wasn't scared. I needed to quieten my puttering heart and flummoxed mind. I needed to understand what had happened, what was happening and the why of it all. Nothing would focus itself and I sat, afraid to move and terrified of staying.

I peeked out the window and saw the usual number of human ants

51 Moments With Fables

crawling along the streets, forty two storeys below … only, they were all headed in the same out-of-city direction. This manic march of madness stunned me. Calm and hurried, it was both surreal and suspicious.

A song played in my head: "Where have all the followers gone? Gone to graveyards everyone!"

I knew I had to make a decision and looked at the politely swarming beetles, slowing perceptively, and knew that a crowd-trap was not my choice. In a solid building, sheltered from the elements and with warmth, light and a well-stocked fridge, I had greater faith. Having made a decision, for good or ill, I felt better and marched out to the reception desk to cover the ghastly silence with noise.

I turned on the radio and set it at full volume over the loud speakers. I was momentarily comforted by human voices but it soon stopped. Just an electronic crackle, amplified in the crazy stillness. I whipped the dial around, desperate for a human sound from any station. They were all silent – just the white noise of a dying world.

Then I heard it. One word. Was it the start of a cut-off sentence or just a word? A name? As the radio stations of the world turned to white noise, a name screamed at me and around the building: "HAL!"

As the sudden silence taunted me, the snow started to fall outside and the shaking began …

On A Quiet Street

On a quiet street where nobody meets is a broken no parking sign and the peeling paint on a fire hydrant that's flecked with pigeon shit. The graffiti artists haven't bothered to visit for a while and the drains are lined with sodden leaves and the spindly bones of a long-dead bird.

There's no paper or rubbish as it's been blown or rotted away after the people left. Even the dogs don't scavenge here anymore for the up-turned rubbish bins are empty, but for the black, dried up banana skins and chewing gum stuck to their insides.

The autumn leaves fall, dry out and blow away, leaving some to choke the drainage grills. Then, when the rains come – as they do more frequently than the shitting pigeons – the gutters overflow, flood the street, leaving lines of grime on the sadly flaking plaster walls that guard the innocent pavement.

The rain has not been for days and small, bitter flotsam resents that the wash has left it behind to stick uselessly to lamp posts and derelict phone booths. Nothing stirs, save a rat's twitching whiskers as it wonders how it found itself in a wasteland of such meagre pickings.

In a world of technology and surveillance, it was the perfect place to meet but logic caves into emotion as I'm tempted to take my feet away as fast and as I sneakily can. But stay I must for this meeting is my final hope, a hope scattered and enfeebled by sagging disappointment and a certainty – the only certainty I know – that the downhill slide is my only way out of this world. But Hope's feeble light forces itself through my sodden, grey blanket of doom. It asks, it beseeches, that I stay for this meeting at the cross-roads to nowhere.

I think I was early but, by now, it feels like he's late. I nod menacingly at Hope and mutter, "I told you so." Hope smiles wanly and a surge of reassurance shimmers through me and I wait some more, not daring to lean against anything lest I get grime on my suit.

Besides, apart from waiting here, I have little to do beyond staying in the shadows and beyond the searchlights of authorities and creditors.

It was a long way to fall, from my ego to my humility, and I didn't fall gracefully. In fact, it damned well hurt and I'm still wincing from the pain of those few months ago.

It wasn't a day I could ever have imagined though, a few days ago, someone on TV had suggested the unconscious fear of this day is what kept me fighting for so long … fighting to climb the ladder, fighting to build my empire and then another empire and another, all to keep the baying wolf of fear away from the largest, thickest, most expensive oak doors that shekels could buy. But what do people on TV know, especially ones wanting more glory than the news they're reporting? This hidden unconscious twaddle is just weirdy, lala New Age claptrap, made up to peddle to the hopeless and gullible. Besides, if anything was hiding, it was doing a damned fine job. My mind's as sharp as a needle and I know exactly what's going on in there all the time – only what I put there.

Anyway, there I was, on the up and up, putting distance between the failures who said I'd never make it and the failure they thought I was who made it.

But then it looked like the ladder I'd been climbing was leaning against the wrong wall. Without warning the dominos started falling, one by one, clinkety clink, accelerating as they knocked each other to the floor. First a rumour; then a call from a worried creditor; then an employee leaking secrets; then my lawyer suggesting (with ice on his voice) I not say anything to anyone; then the media on the line and at my back door and I told them to fuck off. Well, that didn't work as they made up fables from their factless world to make up for their lack of news but, once printed, took on the stature of The Word of God. Denial just encouraged them to fabricate more newspaper-selling stories so I threatened to sue the buggers and they lapped it up like a masochistic boxer who's fired to greatness by the pain inflicted on him. Maybe I should have listened to my lawyer.

In fact, I didn't take it at all at the start, with large daily doses of denial and continual outpourings of blame and justification. They all helped numb me from the pain, from the failure, and that worked for a while. But just for a while.

They were clamouring and barking for my blood, for my money and for their revenge and, for a time, I had the money to pay my lawyer to plug the system with diversions and contrivances. But the money ran out and so did the lawyer. And so here I am, waiting at the end of the line for a character I've never met to guide me to my next lurching post. God knows, I've run out of options and so I wait.

And there he was as if he'd been there all along. Perhaps he had. Maybe I'd been too engrossed to notice the one who could save me, though the likely pain of his saving could be more than I could bear. Perhaps I didn't want to see him so I didn't.

His grim mouth told no secrets and his fine coat, flapping as if to reach his patent leather shoes – and not quite reaching them – subtly reveals a conservative but expensive grey suit; the edges ironed sharply and perfectly cleaned. The person I used to be.

"You haf za money?" he asked quietly, his unmoving face a mask of placidity.

"Money?" I stammered. "That's my problem; I don't have any."

"Mmm, zo I understand." I wasn't sure if this was a dark joke or a check on my honesty. Or something else. "What do you have to barter, then?" His thick lips crept towards a smile. Or was it a grimace?

"I have my desperation and my ingenuity," I proffered, hoping he'd appreciate my reference to Oscar Wilde's quote about having nothing to declare but his genius. He missed the brilliant but ill-timed joke and I prayed his hands weren't around a weapon of some sort, in those deep pockets.

"I do not come to zis schidt hole for nussing." This was a statement, not a question. His right hand moved slightly in his deep, dark pocket. I pretended not to think he was massaging a pistol by looking into his implacable, brown eyes. I suspected he was bald under his black fedora then realised that knowledge didn't help me one bit.

"I thought you could help me. Gerard said …" I said, trying desperately to keep my voice even and low. I don't think I succeeded as it sounded like someone else's; disconnected from me.

"Gerard says many sings. Vot is important is vot I say, huh?"

"Yes, of course."

"Zo, vot can ve exchange, mein friend?"

"I have no money …"

"Vot can ve exchange is the question. Not vot we cannot exchange."

"Yes, I see," I said, seeing very little right now.

"Your ingenuity you tell me of. What is it coming up vith?"

"Not a lot right now," I said, unable to grin in embarrassment. And in fear.

"Vee haf little time and my patience, he is falling into za gutter," he said, quietly. His right hand became a fist in his pocket.

"Look, I'm at the bottom and, right now, I can't think what I have to give," I said, hoping honesty was good for my soul … and for his temper. "I have made millions and, given a chance, I can do it again. I just need a break."

"A break or a breaking leg?" His mouth twitched as if it was contemplating a smile and then resisted it.

"Oh Jesus!" I said hoarsely. "I thought you could help me at the bottom, somehow. That's what Gerard …"

"Forget zis Gerard, shall ve?" he said leaning forward slightly. I could smell garlic on his breath and leant back. "You must haf some vay you can repay my kindness, huh?" Another statement, not a question.

"Everything I had is gone."

"Not vot Gerard says, ya."

Bloody Gerard. Says too much. I thought I could trust him.

"I do have one small investment …"

"Mmm," he said and his uncertain smile didn't falter this time. He knew all the time, I suspected. "Not a worthwhile investment, I'll vager."

As the smile slid from his face, my heart skipped a beat … missed several beats. Bile rose in my throat and I knew his patience was gone, as was my last chance. I'd pushed his boundaries and flattened his fences. God knows, I'd pushed my boundaries for I had no idea what I'd done and what his boundaries were … or what to do now. Against the wall and nowhere to hide, I had no choice – give up, take what was coming and accept my powerlessness.

But could I do that? Could I give up the control I had … or what little I had left?

"So what can I offer?" I asked, desperate for an answer to his threatening questions.

"Let me sink," he said. It was clear he knew his answer but he intended to prolong the suspense. "You have nothing. No stuff. No toys. Nothing to offer that I can carry away, huh?"

"Nothing." I dared not offer any more words than I needed to; words he could trip me up on.

"Zo, there must be something …"

"I'm willing …" I volunteered, not sure what else to say.

"You're willing?" he asked as his face lit up and his hands flew out of his pockets and opened like a flower. His pockets were empty. There was no weapon. I relaxed, feeling quite stupid.

"Yes," I said, stupidly, not sure what the excitement was about.

"When you're villing – just a little villingness – to go to za bottom, to lose it all, to admit zat you're there and zen ask for help. Dat's ven za help arrives. Ven you pretend you're alright, all hokey dokey pretending happy, you're on your own. Ven you're honest and villing, we're here to help."

He was not, of course, a real person but someone in my mind that I conversed with. When I became honest with myself, I was able to become honest with everyone else … eventually. And when I was willing to accept the reality of where I was – the midday person, so to speak – all the help in the world arrived.

Only a fool resides in the dawning time; a time where sleep-blurred eyes creak open to the vague and shifting colours of a slowly wakening world; a time when indistinct shapes merge and mingle, unsure if they're this or that. The slowly dawning mind, still detaching from mystical dreams, is unsure which is dream and which is dawn.

In the dawning life a fool can pretend one thing or another. He thrives in sleep-encumbered fickleness where a million truths fight and snap at each other in the shadow-plays where being right is paramount. Despite the fact that opposing truths are everywhere right, there is solace in clinging to the sinking flotsam of a truth devoid of substance, of veracity. These mutable truths, dodging and weaving from facts and evaporating in the stark glare of sunlight, are kept hidden and nurtured in the mutable blur of a dawning, yawning world.

This is the world I lived in and I loved it – the chameleon I was could hide at will and become what others wished at any time.

Lies were believed, credit was easy and the quick-sand of morals was fun to play in, as long as I kept a solid branch nearby, to pull me out of the mud, to stop me being totally sucked in.

My trusty branch was a belief in God, a desire to know God (or myself) more deeply. It was a quest for peace and contentment and it wasn't always close by. Many times I sunk to my chin, about to take my last gritty breath when I remembered my Call to Peace.

A fool's contrariness loves to test the limits, to push himself to the edge of safety. I developed a need for drama, for a spectacular scene, and this became my code for survival. Boredom was avoided at any cost – usually via that of physical, mental and/or financial pain. Relationships were expendable, my body was indestructible and others' lives and assets existed for my continuing delectation.

But something happened. I'm not sure if it was the last business and relationship break-up or if they were the final stages of a rising call for all of this to be over. The deceit gnawed at my gut and I slowly discovered that the Greg Cousins that I had once known with certainty, had evaporated into a thousand false droplets of fog.

It was time to pull myself together and my aching soul – yearning for oneness and integrity – pulled the magnificent stunt by creating a collapse my selfish pretence could not recover from. It had to go.

I'd had Enough … no, not the enough that gives in to artifice again and again but the ENOUGH that knows no backsliding.

The process of becoming real, of pulling myself together, was one I'd feared … feared so much I'd avoided it by returning to the quick-sand of dawning time. However, this time, the ENOUGH said, "Whatever the pain, whatever the shame, whatever the blame, I'm willing to take the dreaded journey in order to arrive back with me. With Peace. With Contentment."

The dreaded transformation process from back-slide to front-up was easier than expected but it did require constant vigilance, second by second observance of my reactions and thought. That was exhausting, at first, and I slid easily on to the old tram lines, rutted deep from years of traffic. However, day by diligent day, the tiny, focussed vigilance brought me back from the abyss and into the midday sun where all is stark, clear and distinguishable; where Truth is only that without exception, only that which is eternal and that which brings the undeniable feeling of Peace. Excitement doesn't last but Contentment does and the lasting is where I intend to spend my days.

She'd been stunned by his description and honesty and, while her heart tried to absorb the breadth of his pilgrimage, her analytical mind wanted something firm to hook into.

"You'd said love was gentle, giving and strong," she said. "But how can strong be gentle?"

"The brittle oak breaks in the hurricane while the soft palm bends and remains," he said. "Love doesn't fight what is. It accepts and allows. It wishes no change on anyone."

"So, if I'm unfaithful and you love me, you'll accept that?"

"No, I'll accept your behaviour as it is and have no need to change you," he said. "I might stay or I may go. Whatever action I choose, I'll chose it with acceptance of what is, what's actually happening. I won't chose it with bitterness or anger for they come from a demand that something be different from what it is."

"You'll accept me but walk away?" she asked as confusion started to clear … just a little.

"Okay, let's put it this way," he said, his green eyes smiling as he laid a hand gently on hers. "There are only two types of action possible in this world. They are acts of love and calls for love. Calls for love usually hurt someone; usually the caller more than anyone else. Love answers every call for love – every hateful action – with an act of love. In this case, in the face of adultery, the act of love may be to walk away."

"You wouldn't be shitty?"

"Well, ideally, no," he said, chuckling. "I am human and I do fall back into human ego reactions sometimes. I might have moments of bitterness, sadness, regret and so on. In fact, I definitely would. However, each time one of those arose, I'd accept the negative feeling as it came to me, I'd feel it and then let it go, returning to the Love that I am."

"Returning to love?"

"Reminding myself that love isn't personal and nor are acts of love."

"Not personal? Everything's personal!"

"Okay, if you call me an idiot, it's not because I am one. It's because you think you are," he said, patiently. "If we don't like our thoughts of self-hatred – and we all have them – we'll try to throw them at others – a call for love."

"Is this the projection you've talked about?"

"Exactly. So, if we have an argument, we're coming from our little human egos, projecting our little hateful selves at one another. Love flows through all of that – ever present and never changed, like a surf-board through the waves."

"So who wins?"

"No one wins. Only love wins," he said, squeezing her hand gently. "When we choose to remember who we really are – Love, Children of God, the Christ, Buddha or whatever term you want – we release the projections, accept our self-hatred and let it go. Then we return to the peace that was always there."

"Love never goes …" she said, musing.

"Only hate comes and goes, sneaking about disguises of passion and strength. Think of the people who are forever remembered for their greatness – they're the ones who acted in love. The memory of the bearers of hate live with us less peacefully and less eternally. Hate flares up and dies. It is weak and fickle. Love is strong – softly, grace-fully strong.

"I'm not sure I get all this, just yet, but maybe I will."

"You will," he said with assurance. "WE all do, eventually. In the meantime, our little egos will fight against it with every insanity imag-inable. The ego loves drama and hates peace."

"We're a weird lot, aren't we," she said, feeling love rising again.

"We surely are," he said, smiling as he reached over and touched her lips …then, in that moment, they ended up touching lots of other parts of each other.

The Elephant

When a man unsheathes his pen,
The whole world knows what he's doing next.
He opens his soul and reveals his secrets,
In every paragraph and word of text.

Some call him stupid, some say brave,
But the two are the self-same thing, you see,
For stupid is what other people do,
And brave is the same damned thing, done by me.

Like the elephant that towers above the rest,
Not afraid to stand out, be seen and teach us,
This tower of strength, this determined plodder,
Is also the gentlest and kindest of creatures.

Writing a book is a long and lonely journey,
Plodding on alone, self-doubts and many restarts.
But forever is a long time, I know,
That your words will live and touch our hearts.

Many see writers as aloof, sure and intellectual,
But I see you as brave and tireless, beyond hours.
I thank you for your great message, your story,
And your inspiration of strength, oh brother of ours.

(Written to David Gau-Ghan on his 40th birthday, a week before his first book, *The Blue Star*, was printed - published by the famous Bradbury World of Words)

Asharif

In the boat with Asharif are three very wealthy and elegantly dressed people. The man has a grand hat and many layers of flowing robes, while the women are dressed in much lace and silk, with delicately embroidered parasols.

As Asharif rows, he doesn't think about the disparity between these sophisticated people, with their fine talk and smooth skin, and his own blunt manner and blistered hands. These people of high standing may be comparing their impeccably buckled shoes with his bare feet, their flowing garments with his tattered shirt and shorts, the large jewels on their fingers with his broken and dirty fingernails. Asharif could have looked at these outer differences if he'd chosen, but his interest was in that which lay beneath the human veneer. This is why these people chose his above all the other water taxis.

Some of the other water taxis were very beautiful craft, with brightly coloured paint in intricate patterns and scrolling words. Some gleamed in the bright sunlight and were decorated with streamers, bells and garlands of flowers. Many of the taxi-men wore what we might call uniforms - smart clothing of particular colours and patterns that matched their boats. Most of them were well groomed and, despite the hard physical work, kept themselves very clean. Many of them practised speeches and phrases and were able, after some time, to imitate the language, tone and gestures of their educated customers.

There was, it seemed, a common idea that the cleaner, smarter and more clever you were, the more customers you could get, enabling you to make enough money to sell your boat and live in a manner that more closely resembled your customers. It was not possible, of course, for taxi-men to ever become society-men, for the brand of their birth could never be erased or exchanged. However, a taxi-man could always, with foresight, perseverance and ingenuity, become a manservant or horseman - positions which meant less physical work and more contact with the "people of society". Somehow, the unspoken belief was that the more contact one had with people of society, the more likely one could become one - almost as if their wealth, silks, jewels and powders would rub off. It never did but all lived in hope.

For the society people, there was an unspoken belief that the less contact one had with the "lower elements of society", the less chance one had of becoming (at least fractionally) like them. Most society people, then, chose the more colourful craft and the most "cultured" taxi-men.

So why did this unkempt Asharif prosper so much? In a tidy-but-un-painted boat, in purely functional and slightly tattered clothes and with an accent and manner quite unchanged from birth, he should have been the poorest of the taxi-men. But he wasn't. Further, instead of actively engaging his customers in bright and enthusiastic conversation, he as-siduously avoided saying anything unless asked to do so. Yes, he was polite, but it was as if he didn't care. And yet, through the layers of cosmetics, jewellery and clothing that surrounded and protected these society people, some particular ones among them felt that he actually cared more than anyone else they knew. While Asharif's outer appear-ance and behaviour belied his caring, it was plainly evident to a small number of them.

Obviously, most society people would choose not to travel with Asharif, the plain and sullen one and, initially, he sat at the wharf for hours while the more splendid craft plied their trade with vigour. This seemed not to bother Asharif, who simply sat and waited, as if knowing of some divine event on its way. Then, once in a while, a society-per-son or group, feeling a little adventurous, would deliberately choose the taxi that no one else would, perhaps hoping to have more to boast about than others of a more conservative nature.

Most of these adventurous passengers had a need of noise, hustle and bustle. Asharif's silence would unnerve them and they'd have to fill the space with chatter. Eventually they'd have to risk the taboo of talking to the lower people - they'd comment on the weather or some other irrelevancy and he would nod and, maybe, smile. If nothing needed to be said, he said nothing. In desperation they would (in their need to fill the silence with noise) ask a question which he would have to answer.

So, after deep thought (as deep as they were capable) they might ask a question about marriage and Asharif would tell them that the man they were about to marry was actually in love with another particular lady (who he'd name) and that their impending marriage would last 3½ years and end in bankruptcy and misery. Or they might ask something about politics and he'd tell them who the next Shamir (or Governor) would be, what he would do and what effect that would have in their businesses. Or they'd ask about health and he'd reassure them that their father's terrible illness would soon be gone and that full health would be restored in seven weeks, if they administered a particular herbal concoction to him.

Whatever subject they alluded to, he would know, somehow, of their personal concerns and future and, without discrimination, he'd simply give the facts. As time went by, they realised that he was never wrong. In time he came to be respected, though many first thought of him as a charlatan and felt bound to test him. He never faltered and his answers were equally caring, dispassionate and accurate for all questioners, no matter how cynical, aggrieved or wide-eyed they were.

Without looking, it was as if he could see into their hearts and know the real questions they were afraid to ask. Then, in the same way, he seemed able to look into their souls and their futures and give answers from the heart of one who was incapable of judgement. He seemed unable to judge people by their dress or behaviour, and unable to judge the impact of that which he told. As a messenger, he dispassionately delivered his messages with no thought of softening or "adjusting" them to the sensitivity of the listener.

And yet there came with these (sometimes) harsh messages, an overwhelming sense of caring and compassion. Even the most difficult-to-swallow pills were rendered sweetly edible. Though he volunteered no advice, if a wise questioner asked for advice around his or her future, the counsel was ever wise and reassuring.

By attraction rather than advertising, then, Asharif became a very busy man. Though he might have rowed all day, he always had time for another customer - his energy was boundless. Sometimes he would be spared that hard work as a customer, trying to get to the bottom of a major problem, would ask him to stop rowing and to simply advise. Often this plain craft could be seen quietly drifting with the tide while the more garish and noisy taxi-men ploughed through the water with great gusto and a little envy.

And, in the middle of the harbour, bobbing in the wake of other water traffic, large amounts of gold and jewels would be proffered in grateful thanks for the knotty problem solved. Asharif never refused these gifts, accepting them with the same simple "thank you" that accompanied the compliments for him. He did, however, turn down other offers. Sometimes he would be offered a position as an advisor for a nobleman and, always, he'd decline. It was as if he wanted to remain available to all, without discrimination - to be the exclusive property of one (no matter how wealthy) was not his way.

At times, an astute observer might see a thankful customer alight from the humble craft and know that changes were afoot. Within a week the people would be astounded at the brilliance of some political or business initiative, and all their lives would be enhanced a little. While the masses would shower this ingenious politician or business-man with their approval, two or three people would smile and nod to each other, knowing where the seed of the progressive changes really started. Asharif was never acknowledged for his part in any of the happenings and one suspects that's how he would have wanted it.

He plied his trade untiringly, provided his truth when asked, accepted that which his customers offered, offended no one and remained in the simple integrity of who he really was. A more innocuous man could not be imagined and all who knew him well, grew to love him.

For some reason, though, some were not happy with him. Many speculated on whether it was a jealous taxi-man, a jilted lover, a dishonest politician or a greedy businessman, but we'll never know the real culprit. An uproar ensued after his boat was found floating in the middle of the harbour. On closer inspection, his body was found face-up, with his arms and legs nailed to the wooden seats, while his craggy and serene face smiled at the peaceful sky above. Several official inquiries were instigated but no offenders were discovered, though two taxi-men and three politicians were found to have left the city abruptly.

There was a mass wailing for the loss of this simple man and different groups began to frantically create books from the words that had been remembered from his boat trips. There was, of course, bickering between these groups of Asharifts (as they called themselves) as to who was the authentic group and who had the most accurate accounts of his life. That bickering continues today and while they may focus on proving themselves the most righteous and the chosen ones, they forget that whatever version of the Asharif story is believed, it provides a profound understanding of life and it enables many confused, pained and anxious people to realize the power and beauty they have within.

Strangely, his death meant that he now lives eternally, forever carrying people across the harbour of their doubt and fear, to the safe harbour of their peace, joy and acceptance.

Three Scrawny Minutes

This is the song I wrote to sing at my father's funeral. Sadly, I left it too late to work out the chords and, anyway, I was only allowed to talk for three minutes and the song would have gone for longer.

To sum up a man's life in three scrawny minutes or less
To curse him, swear at him, thank him and bless
That's what they gave me as his body lay here
And I hadn't to think where I start, the far or the near
For memories spawn memories, lever open broken doorways
And there's another in its shadow, not far away

Chorus
So how do you talk when he's flat in a box
Lying still, stupid suit and new socks
This ain't the man who strode the earth, no fear
With a mind alert and a temper to match, beware
It's my old dad, you silly bastards, you can't be told
Too big to fit small words, small spaces, small church won't hold
Smoking and striding, thinking and yelling, dogs at heel
The hills poured their soul into a man who wouldn't feel

We've come a long way, this old man and me
From a young father with a child on his knee
To the sadness, the weakness of brain tumour and broken heart
And me the young boy; once close, now grown apart
I might talk of sad times, glad times and the urbane
But from here, this great distance, they're one and the same

Chorus

I remember the five o'clock starts as the sun yawned awake
Seven men, seven horses, twenty dogs in the day-break
Rolling smokes, creaking saddles, snuffing dogs and still trees
Dust rising as magpies ripped the silence, if you please
But the men nodded, murmured and said bugger all
Sucked on their fags, eased leather straps, heard the hills call

Chorus

One by one we'd break from the group
Till there was him and me, horses and dog troupe
A rising, weird feeling he wanted to talk as fathers do
He'd grunt and ahem, looking shy then give orders anew
Horse riding in rain, sun or wind, there's no one for miles
Lambing ewes, fixing fences, he's never far and I smiles

Chorus

For when the horses are shod, the dogs are fed and the day is over
What's to be said in those thousands of acres, sheep in clover
Gnarled hands, leathered faces and cracked smiles
Tell all in their silence, their stoic pain, than all of the miles
Of kind words, cute stories, so banal to impress
Shoved neatly into three scrawny minutes or less

Chorus

You see, a boy and a man grow through each other in tune
They hate and love, curse and joke, chuckle and fume
But there's nothing to be said, the story in our heart
'Cause there's good and bad, tough and sweet, dumb and smart
Three scrawny minutes, scrawny words get in the scrawny damned
    way
Life grown together, apart, and no one's gone home to stay

Chorus

The Wimp

I
n a land of sporting heroes there lived a boy who wasn't very interested in sport. While the other children were talking about Andy
Maloney or the High Flyers or the Scull Crushers or whoever, he
was wondering who they were or what they did. He would hear the
others talking excitedly about how their school team thumped another
team and he would feel the pain of being thumped. He would over-
hear the radio or the television and it was so exciting (apparently) that
the Fangers had annihilated the Head Hitters, or Fred (Fists) Fury had
knocked out Clubber Jones, or the Unglish XI had "wiped the mat"
with the Ondian side, or the brilliant Old Zealand sailors had trounced
the arrogant Ometican ones and all the losers were trampled in the
rush to congratulate the winners. This poor boy could not feel any of
the excitement - he just felt sick thinking of being pummelled, beaten,
slaughtered and butchered. That people voluntarily went out to do that
to others made him wonder - perhaps he was odd as everyone else
seemed to enjoy it.

It always seemed that the winning team or person was brilliant,
clever, tough, fit and wonderful in some way while the losers were
always arrogant, a rabble, pathetic and weak. This seemed odd as the
next week the tables could be turned and all of the adjectives would
have to be swapped around.

Because this sporting talk made him feel quite sick he didn't join
in much with others. He found that if you weren't a real sports fanatic
(which they equated with being a real sports person) then you were
branded with the worst adjective that could be applied to any creature

- worse than that applied to any losers. You were a wimp and this is what he was called - The Wimp.

This Wimp found his enjoyment more with the things that man did not create and his conversations were with himself and those non-human things - animals, birds, plants, mountains, rivers, sunshine and other quiet things.

He was lucky that his parents had both been good at sport and they did not try to make up for any deficiency in themselves by forcing him to be sporty. His mother loved her garden and his father enjoyed the forest so he learned a lot about nature from them.

However, he found that nature taught him a whole lot more. The conversations he had with the birds and animals grew quieter and quieter as time went on. He found that if he was really quiet, nature actually answered his questions. He was sitting down one day, watching a Black Bird and wondering how nature could hear him if he was really quiet. Immediately an answer came into his head:

"I am talking to you with no sound and you can hear me, can't you?"

The Black Bird seemed to be looking at him but wasn't chirping. The Wimp smiled, shook his head and wondered if he was 'hearing things'.

"Yes you are," came the immediate reply in his head, "You are hearing me, the Black Bird. We are talking as all of us birds talk - from mind to mind. It is much quicker and can be used over longer distances than can voicing. We just use our voices to cheer up the world with song and to protect our young from non-bird people. Is there anything else you would like to know?"

The Wimp wondered if he was going mad and why he had suddenly started hearing this inside voice.

"No, you are not going mad at all," came the words before he even realised what his own thoughts were. "You are very sane. You can hear me because you have stopped to listen. We have always been here to talk with, but most people think that communication is only sending their message out. Very few stop to listen and listening is the other half of communication. Communication only works if both halves are there. We are very thankful that you have stopped to listen."

As time went on The Wimp found that he could talk in his head to all sorts of beings - birds, deer, cats, dogs, cows, possums and even trees, flowers and a river. He didn't try to talk to any of them but just found, in a quiet moment, words coming into his head. Somehow he could also know what was sending the words. Trees talked differently from dogs, dogs were different from bees and so on.

He really enjoyed these conversations as the things nature said were so nice. It was always polite and never said anything nasty about anyone. If someone was not very good, it was explained in such an understanding and accepting way. He also learned a lot - what the weather would be tomorrow, where things he lost were, what things made him really happy and when to go home so he was never late. Sometimes they would help with school projects and things others wanted to know. These nature people seemed to know more about him than he did, but he didn't mind. They were so nice about it all. They never complained, or insulted you, or sulked, or swore. Just pleasant, positive and friendly.

Sometimes his nature friends wouldn't talk to him and he soon discovered that it was because he had too much on his mind - their words couldn't fit in. If he stopped thinking too hard or stopped worrying and left a space in his brain, their words would come in loud, clear, friendly and helpful.

The Wimp's teachers began to notice little changes in him. His school-work began to improve (which was about time as it was awful before) and his shy nature became like a flower and slowly opened and he showed more confidence. He even started contributing to class discussions, which he had never done before. Sometimes he seemed to know things that children just didn't know, and even things that most adults didn't know.

His sports teacher also noticed gradual changes. The Wimp knew he was getting fitter than the others as while they were watching sport on television, swapping basketball cards and talking about their latest hero he was walking in the forest, running with the animals and swimming in the river that told him about himself before he was born and other amazing things. But he couldn't bring himself to tell his teacher about his 'training'.

The other children noticed small changes too. Instead of being very shy and a bit moody he became .... well .... nice. Not smart or clever, but helpful and friendly to everyone, even if they weren't nice to him. When someone insulted him he just smiled and carried on with what he was doing. He also complimented people on little things and they liked that.

One day one of the boys thought he would show-up The Wimp and asked him what the score would be for next week's rugby match. Without even thinking, The Wimp found his mouth saying 23-15 to the Budgers. He didn't even know how rugby was scored or who the Budgers were. The strange thing was that the score was 23-15 to the Budgers! Nobody was more astounded than The Wimp.

But he wasn't only astounded. He was also a little scared. How was he to know what a score could be? Was it coincidence? He was too scared to find out. It was as if some really intelligent person had taken over his brain for a few seconds, and that didn't feel good.

Of course, the other children wanted to test him again and asked him all kinds of future things. He politely and firmly said 'no'. They went away a little sulky, calling him other things besides Wimpy - like selfish, useless, pathetic and dummy. The names were the least of his problems. He really wanted to know what was going on and didn't know of anyone to talk to.

As it happened, the next weekend his grandparents arrived and his Grandmother took him aside and said:

"I hear you have created quite a stir at school. Do you want to talk about it?"

A huge smile crossed his face and he blurted out everything - his fears, his conversations, the voices in his head and that, aside from the confusion, he was feeling calmer and more peaceful in himself. Why he told her anything at all he didn't know, but he just did - and she listened with a quiet and knowing smile.

She asked him why he thought some people could grow plants better than others - people with 'green fingers'. He didn't know.

"Plants are like us," she said. "They like to be loved. The more a person loves their plants, the better they will grow."

That was logical, he thought.

"Why do cats and dogs walk up to some people and not others?" she asked. "Because they can feel, somehow, who is friendly and who is not."

"Well, more and more birds and animals seem to come to me now," he mused aloud.

"That is because you now feel happier and more peaceful," she explained. "They like the feelings you are feeling, just like you do."

That, too, seemed logical. But how do they talk to me, he still wondered.

"Your feelings that they feel are no different from your thoughts," she explained, as if she knew just what he was thinking. "And you feel, in your head, their thoughts in exactly the same way. It only works, though, if you are totally open and honest. If you have any bad or negative thoughts they will block the system and it doesn't work."

"But how can I tell the future," he asked, still worried.

"How do the trees know what the weather will be or how does your cat know where you will find your shoes?" she asked.

He shrugged.

"The answers to everything we need to know are within us all - people, cats, black birds, trees," she said. "If we can slow our minds down, stop the logical thinking and allow a space for the answers to come in, then they will. Some people use meditation, some use music, some use other methods and some can just do it without trying. You seem to be the last sort. Just remember one thing, though, and this is very important. As long as your intentions are the best and for the good of all, you will receive what you need, which is not always what you want. If you want to hurt someone or to do something bad then it could backfire on you. You have a great power within you and make sure you use it wisely. Go and have a think about what I have said and we can talk again some other time."

So he went and he thought and wondered if he was any wiser than before - it seemed that the more he knew, the more there was to know. It was nice, though, to know he wasn't the only one who talked to trees and that there was now someone to discuss these things with. He decided that he would only tell people things if it was going to he really helpful for them. He realised that it was nice being able to boast his ability but it wasn't very positive for anyone. He asked two of his friends (the oak tree and the river) and they agreed that he had made the right decision, so he felt better about it.

This decision caused a few problems at school but he firmly and politely stuck to his decision and ignored the names the others called him. He did find, though, that his mouth would just say things without him wanting it to and he determined to try to control it.

Because he had shown such great improvement in all areas, his teachers wanted to give him a prize at the end of the year. But, as he had not excelled at any one particular thing, there was no prize to give him. So they thought up a new one and at the annual prize-giving he gratefully received the most Well Informed and Mature Pupil prize.

Which is what *Wimp* stands for.

The Invaders

Welcome, Oh Man of the Trees, to our sanctuary, our hill above the sea. We feel your apprehension at stepping on and sitting in this place, for you know it is where many tupuna have laid their cloaks and stepped forth into the world of spirit. Yes, it is tapu and we thank you for asking permission and acknowledging our presence and our space. It is tapu to those with a different coloured skin from your own and we feel your uncertainty (though not fear) of being called here. You may have a lighter coloured skin but it is not that, but the colour of your heart that we see - a heart that loves this land and all lands, our Papatuanuku. We feel your uncertainty but we do welcome you and ask that you share our message - a message for the changing times, a message that may surprise some.

You, with your respect for our space and our beliefs, may see this sacred hill as ours and belonging to no others. That is how it was but now times are changing. This hill, this Aotearoa, this Papatuanuku, does not belong to anyone any longer. So who does it belong to, you may ask. We cannot answer that for the question is asked the wrong way around. You might like to ask who do you, we or any other be-ing here belong to and we would say they all belong to Papatuanuku, Mother Earth. This belonging is not, however, an ownership of another but a nurturing of another.

You think, Mr Tree Man, that you would like to plant trees in the desert places so that you can heal and nurture our Earth Mother. We, and your Mother, would encourage you to do that and for each step you take in that direction, know that there would indeed be many thousands in spirit who would also take steps to guide and help your way in this. We would, though, remind you that this healing or nurturing is never a one-way process. As vital as this healing is for our Mother, so it is for you and those with whom you work and travel. The trees and your love for our Mother, our Papatuanuku, will help heal her, but as you take your plans and your inspiration to the Aborigines to heal the Mother's lungs, or to the Indians on Turtle Island to heal her heart and backbone, so you will raise the self-worth of yourself and those others. The creative and cooperative effort of working together for a common goal will engender many lasting friendships and will inspire all to realise that they can do something positive and lasting, as does the cooperative effort in trying to save a beached whale.

We do not want to belittle your efforts, but know that without them, Papatuanuku has, in her immense power, the ability to do her own healing. But the efforts of her children are always appreciated and make her job a little easier. As with your own dear mother, she was able to cope very well with all of her tasks when you were a child. But if you helped with a few dishes or fed the cat or did other small tasks, she was very appreciative and sometimes rewarded you. She may have also been quick to reprimand you when you hindered her or misbehaved. So, too, our Great Mother does not appreciate her progress and growth being hindered and has and will have reason to reprimand, in her own way, those who do not acknowledge and appreciate her essence and her growth.

The great power of our Mother Earth is not appreciated by most of her human children and, here, we get back to our first words which were that this land is not anyone's exclusively. Our Mother knows who should be where, and in her subtle and powerful way ensures that the right inhabitants are drawn to the right places, at all times. This may not seem so but we ask you, first, to look at your own land and see the objections to the many new immigrants from Asian lands. Many do not see this as being right but we simply say that if it is happening, then it is right. If it were not right, our Mother would have it happen otherwise. Many of you from Aotearoa may see these immigrants as not being appreciative and not in accord with your values, especially towards the land. We would want to say two things here:

Firstly, an honest look at your own dealings with the land may show much destruction, desecration, pollution and wastefulness and, perhaps, these immigrants are reflecting and magnifying your own thoughts and behaviour.

Secondly, if these immigrants are disrespectful and wasteful of the land (we have no judgement here, the judgement is yours alone) they may be doing you and our Mother a favour by accelerating your thoughts and moves to be more kind towards her.

We would also like to point out that every person and race on this planet is a native and an immigrant, so who should have first rights to any space?

And so you sit amongst the peace and quiet of the trees, hearing the noise and crashing of the sea below. And so it always is - the movement must come to the stillness for each to be appreciated in their own ways.

Throughout history there have been invasions of gentle and peaceful people by savage and aggressive invaders and the Vikings may be a good example. Some may feel that the gentle people of England did not deserve to be invaded by those savage and uncaring marauders and if Mother Earth is orchestrating all this then she must be very unfair. But perhaps the Celts had become too insular and apathetic and this "reseeding" was necessary to add vitality to a complacent race. It may have stopped them squabbling amongst themselves and engendered a cooperative spirit to defend their land and to appreciate their beautiful space a little more.

And so, throughout history, this reseeding has always been a function of the growth of this planet and its children. Sometimes the reseeding was done very consciously by the humans, as did the Waitaha (before the Maoris) and many other groups who listened closely to the Mother. Sometimes the Mother had to enforce the reseeding herself and it may have seemed unfair.

So who is running this show, this life of yours, this planet of yours, you may well ask. And we would answer, "all of you." The Mother and her children are all running it. To clarify this answer we ask that you look to your own mother and see that she thought only of you and your growth and development, sometimes to her detriment. Sometimes she punished you and it seemed unfair. You now know that the punishment could cause her pain and advance your growth. When you listened, obeyed and helped, you were rewarded. She was learning and growing herself through all the joys and pains of your childhood. Always, though, she was there with her love and caring and her overview was greater than yours.

So, too, with Mother Earth. We need say no more.

Glossary of Maori words:

Aotearoa   *New Zealand*
Papatuanuku *Mother Earth*
Tapu   *Sacred, special*
Tupuna   *Dead ancestors*
Waitaha   *The people in New Zealand before the Maoris arrived*

The Island of Cinnamon

Once upon another time, sweet friends, when dreaming was worth it and futures weren't planned, there stood an island, its back to the Land of Past across the watery waste. Once upon this island, sweet friends, were people with exotic tastes and voracious appetites for life. Though this time was before your history books, it is, indeed, etched into your cells and souls, forwarded on by the genes of your in-laws and outlaws.

These ebullient and peaceful people had no use for memories for their glee was in now, in this present moment. And this present moment … and every present moment to come, on the Island of Nowt. Mistakes were not sins but errors, opportunities to learn anew. There were no failures, only graduates, and they often and spontaneously held ceremonies in glad celebration of another soul's adventurous learning. These gladuation ceremonies were community events where old and young would gather in noisy, colourful abandon to congratulate the error-finder for bridge-walking to a new understanding. And, when all the children were tucked up in bed, there might be some naked rumbly bum in the moonlight's friendly smile, with whoever was at hand. None of the children were sure who their fathers were and all adults acted as parents to all the children.

We might all wonder how anything got done, how houses got built and food got gathered on Nowt Island but it did. Gleefully and simply, tasks were carried out and no one needed reminding of them for nothing was done as work – all was done as peace. We might ponder at their wisdom for while all was provided as needed, fearlessness didn't ask of them to store up for rainy days.

But a rainy day came, the day your history books started. A strange craft from across the water beached itself on the gentle shore and belched out its black clothed tall hatted people. These people from Land of Past, these Pastors, had fixed and sombre faces, dried like old prunes. Their eyes never crinkled and their teeth never showed. The Nowters stepped back as these erect and wooden ones walked through their naked midst.

"Where is your leader?" the first one of Past asked, the one with the tallest hat.

"Leader?" the islanders asked, their minds tasting a new word, found it rancid and spat it out.

"Who's in charge?"

"Charge?" they asked, their minds choking on the second word.

"Your head man, your chief, top man …"

Silence was his answer – a stupefied answer.

"Who makes the decisions, silly people!" he commanded, his dried up face contorting from something unpleasant inside it.

"Decisions?" said a Nowter, trying to help with the poor man's confusion, with the unpleasantness inside him. "No one makes decisions. Decisions make us."

"What … what rubbishychop!" he said, his lips exploding like they weren't coming back. He turned to the other Tall Hatters lined up neatly behind him. Several of them opened and shut their mouths as if to let words out; words that turned back down their throats when they saw the light of day.

Another skulking silence sneaked around and enveloped everyone in its sticky tentacles. Words came up throats and dried to ash on tender tonsils and, for the first time, the islanders of Nowt felt no desire for a party and so quietly walked away.

"B … b … but we need to talk to someone!" blurted out another Pastor, second in the tidy queue.

The islanders stopped and turned, waiting for the talking.

"Who can we talk to?" asked number three in the line, his teeth showing but not in a smile.

The islanders opened their hands, all ready to receive the talking.

"Who, blast it? We need to talk to someone!" demanded Pastor three, his stolid face going quite quaky.

"We are all someone," said the islanders together, as if one voice from one mouth.

"This is stupidy muck! Someone must be in charge, someone must be special ..."

"We are all special," said many people at once.

"All special? Not possible, just crazyhat," said Pastor One, his face recovering from the unpleasantness inside it, somewhat.

The icky silence crawled up again and glued lips together.

"Right, if that's how you want it ..." said Pastor Two.

"Stop! I'm in charge, Number Two," said Number One, looking behind him with gravely unpleasant on his face. He turned back. "So, we're here to give you a sinless God."

"A skinless God?" asked a small boy.

"A sinless God, sinner boy," said Pastor One, looking triumphant, though no one knew what his triumph could be for. Number Two and Four humphed in agreement.

"Thank you for your sinless gift," said many mouths, anticipating another gladuation. "Where is it, please?"

"God is not a gift. God is God," stammered Tall Hat One.

"God is what?" asked a young woman, determined to find understanding in the confusion, another opportunity to graduate.

"God is God. God is good, sinner girl ..."

"Good what is God?"

"Just good." That seemed to be the end of the sinless God explanation and the islanders, as one, looked to the sky, found no clarity in the blue so walked off to prepare for another gladuation ceremony since the answer must surely come if they let it.

The line of Tall Hatters, of Pastors, shuffled forward hesitantly, stopped, looked at itself in dismay and eventually followed the Nowters to their village centre. There they smelt the sinful waft of coffee pass their noses and saw vats of brown boiling badness and platters of evil cakes and savouries, all sprinkled with brown powder, something that was sure to arouse evil thoughts and wicked deeds. They stood aghast as the quietly smiling joy-sayers handed out their mugs of milky coffee and sprinkled upon them this foreign and sinful powder.

This powder, this brown powder was an offence to the stolid nostrils of the men of Past for they knew, they just knew, it was the cause of all the wickedness here ... the nudity, gaiety, touching, lack of prayerful solemnity … all signs of Godless lives. My, how these ignorant savages needed the Religion of Rightness. But how to begin? These people had no structure to pull down, no leader to bargain with, no divisiveness to lever them apart and against each other. They had no interest in listening. They were too happy, abandoned and lascivious. There were no enforcers for there were no laws.

There was no way to bring these sinners to God fearing obedience as they seemed to fear nothing.

Pastor One could only think that he must return to Past defeated, for the first time ever. He commanded his queue to follow him as he turned about and marched back to the gawping door of their craft. Not all turned and followed. In fact, none but Pastor Two and Pastor Four did so. Pastor Four plucked a bowl of brown powder from a table, snuck it under his great-coat and marched off, looking back wistfully.

The history book writer, Pastor Five, remained on the island of Now and so you won't read of this at school. And, since the brown powder came from the sinner man, so it came to be called, though none of the joy it induced in the savages ever reached Pastor Four, to his enduring disappointment.

Mountain-Top Talking

As I stand on the mountain-top, the world looks so small and beautiful; a quiet blue haze. I start on my way down and clumsily dislodge a small rock that clatters and bumps its way down the path ahead of me.

The stillness makes me stop and breathe and admire. There is so much beauty in the quiet and the nothingness. Just brown rugged rocks and smooth blue sky - nothing between us. As I stand I feel that I am both of these at once - brown and rugged, blue and smooth, like the eagle that flies to the heavens and yet sees the smallest detail on the earth below. I can talk to both Ranginui the Sky Father and Papatuanuku, the Earth Mother, in quiet, intimate conversation - the three of us in one circle. These vast beings on either side, and the tiny me between, have a need to talk. We talk without words and this karanga, or thought, conversation is very intense, more serious than I have ever felt before. These great and powerful beings are sad, very sad, and they want my help. My help! This insignificant speck of humanity! What can I do for these timeless and wonderful beings?

As our karanga conversation begins, Ra, the Giver of All Life, acknowledges and thanks his God with a beautiful orange sunrise and then ascends, bright and yellow, to join us. He, too, is sad and needs my help. This trio of vastness and timelessness need my help and I am overwhelmed.

"Yes, we are large and you are small, Dear One," says Ranginui, "but we all need each other's help. It is the size of the giving and not the size of the form that is important."

Feeling their great sadness, the wairua, the spirit, moves me. I have no thought but to help. My smallness fades and I just am; without size, without dimension. I begin to see my essence and their essence and we are all the same - an essence without time or dimension, an essence of nothing but love.

I wonder what I can do, how I can help, what their sadness is. So many questions.

"I have been trampled on, cleaved and dirtied by a being that has no thought of the pain it causes," says Papatuanuku. "My parts have been removed from inside, crushed and spread over the rest of me. And that extraction, that crushing and that spreading have unbalanced me, have dirtied me and have caused great pain. Those parts were needed where they were."

My karanga was of the minerals and the oil in the Earth. Was I right?

"If I took one of your arms and one of your legs off," she continues, with a sigh, "crushed them and then stuck some of the bits over the rest of your body, you would feel three things, as there are three of us here with you now."

"Yes," I think, "I would feel intense pain, I would feel unbalanced and I would feel less effective - less able to fend for myself and less able to help others."

"Correct, Dear One," she says, smiling sadly. "I am sick and as this one continues to gnaw at and to destroy me today, I become more sick. I cannot fend for myself and I cannot feed that which does me damage."

"But why would you want to feed or help someone who hurts you?" I ask, perplexed.

"That is my reason for being, my love," Papatuanuku says, proudly. "I give unconditionally, with love, to all who are with me. That giving is my sustenance, for giving and loving are a circle, if they are unconditional."

"This same being that tears at my sister," says Ranginui, "blankets my being with continuous soot. I am finding it harder and harder to provide Papatuanuku and all her beings with breath."

This soot, I muse, must be the pollution poured into the air.

"Yes, that soot does deplete my essence. It takes my breath and my strength," says Ranginui. "But the worst soot does not come from the burning and transforming of Papatuanuku, but from the mind of this destructive being. It has a mind full of fear, of ownership, of divisiveness and of separateness. It thinks that it is "It" and that other beings are "other" and that its space must always get larger and must be protected. It looks down at its possessions and it takes short breaths and so its thoughts of anger and fear go through my being with a shiver and I am weakened. The love and energy I receive from The Source, through Ra, is sent to Papatuanuku for her and her beings. But that love is weakened through the negative thoughts returning from her, and so we all become less."

"And what is this being you speak of?" I ask. "Is it Man?"

"No," says Ra, glaring brightly, "It is you,"

"Me?" I ask, frightened. "Little me standing here?"

"Yes, you," he says firmly.

"But I haven't polluted or destroyed," I plead. "Negative people do those things. I try to be loving and gentle and giving."

"You are people," says Ra. "You are a person and therefore you are people. There is no separateness. And we are all a part of the all and so we are also people as people are the rocks, the clouds, the burning oil and the poisonous chemicals."

My chest heaves, my tears stream and the responsibility and emotion become too much. I slump to the ground with my heart bursting and my moans echoing down the valley. After a time, the fingers of Ra, rays of sunlight, caress my forehead and a gentler Ra is heard.

"You are also the love and compassion and the best of all of us, Great One," he says quietly.

Silence. Nothing. Peace.

I feel the hurt, the anger and also the love and compassion. I also feel nothing, stillness, silence. I am everything and I am nothing. I am the bright unrelenting Ra, the ever changing and changeless Ranginui and the caring, breathing Papatuanuku. I am also the insignificant me on a mountain-top, overwhelmed by it all. What can I do, how can I help, I wonder again.

"Do not do anything," says Ranginui.

"But how can I make things better," I ask, with dust-streaked tears on my face. "I want to help."

"You are helping right now, Great One," continues Ranginui. "The love and compassion you are expressing right now are healing me. The wairua that moves in you, moves in me and will move through many others."

"Thank you for that, my sky friend," I say, "But there must be something else I can do. I must take some action to help us all."

"No, Dear One," says Papatuanuku, gently. "Look at us. We do not rush around doing. We just be and we must allow others to be."

"But surely I can tell everyone what you have told me," I exclaim.

"No, Dear One," says Papatuanuku. "You must just be and in that being, grow with greater love each day. For then they will come to you for the words, as you have come to us today. Then you can speak and do. Not with advice but by example and with wisdom. And what is wisdom?"

"Wisdom is knowledge," I say, knowingly.

"Wisdom = knowledge + humility," says Ra. "You are no greater or lesser than your pupils or your teachers, as you are no greater or lesser than any of us."

Their humility is moving, perhaps more moving than their wisdom. I stood, bowed, not knowing what to do or think next.

"Look up, Great One," says Ra. "Raise your eyes above your feet and your assets and see the glory of us, the glory that is you."

I do, and feel larger.

"Now breathe," he says. "Long, slow, deep breaths. For breath is life, is love and the essence of your being. Shallow breathing gives a shallow life on this Earth. Deep breathing gives a deep meaning in this life."

I breathe as never before. I feel Ranginui in me, and Papatuanuku and Ra. I become all there is; expanded, powerful and humble.

"Now, Dear One," says Papatuanuku, "you have a journey. Walk down off my shoulder, down to our sister, Tangaroa. There, in her glistening, salty waters, you will meet some friends, the dolphin people. They feel as you do, as we do, the anger, the sadness and the isolation felt by Man, and it burdens them. But they continue to be themselves - playful, loving and positive. They will teach you much. Bathe in Tangaroa and her waters will heal your hurt as will the ethers of Ranginui."

There seems so much to do.

"The damage and sadness was yesterday," says Ra, smiling. "I bring in another day now and live in the essence of that. Tomorrow has not yet dawned so stay from that. In every moment there is very little to do."

I feel lighter, thank them and say goodbye.

"Never goodbye, Great One," says Ranginui. "We are always with you and you are always with us."

I smile and skip a few steps.

It is a long walk down off Papatuanuku's shoulder and as Ra prepares to end another day, I see a village below and stop for a rest. Looking down at the village, I see many people milling around and see that several houses seem to be damaged from a rock-slide.

For some reason I think back to that little rock I had dislodged at sunrise. Surely that hadn't started a rock-slide and caused so much damage and pain. I feel appalled at my silly action and what I might have done.

"Yes, you could have done that, Dear One," says Papatuanuku, with a sigh. "And look how powerful you have become."

I don't feel powerful at all. I feel like a monster.

"No, Dear One," she continues, "you are powerful. You see before you families working together to help each other - families that have fought and argued for years. You have damaged their assets and their bodies, but healed their minds."

I sit and think this over. I cannot bring myself to stand, to walk down and help, much as I want to.

"You have done enough this day," says Ranginui. "Be content, be still."

As Ra creeps over the horizon he acknowledges and thanks the day and his God with an orange spectacle - a sunset of great beauty - as he does every day of his existence.

I thank them all, curl up and sleep in the gentle bosom of Papatuanuku.

Glossary of Maori words

Karanga	*Thought*
Papatuanuku	*Mother Earth*
Ra	*The sun*
Ranginui	*The sky*
Tangaroa	*The sea*

The Boat Takers

It wasn't desperation that urged the men to take the boat, it was a simple knowing that there must be a better way, a better land, a better life. Desperation had been a transient companion to each of these men and it had forced many a hasty action, but desperation never stays to the end. It is always there at the start - the first potato crop failure, the first non-payment by the butcher and the wool merchant, the first week without food, the first child to die, the first burglary, the first arrest – then it finds another to befriend. After your family, farm and dignity have been taken by the Grim Reaper, the landlord, the law and the hard hand of an oppressor, desperation quietly leaves and acceptance and resignation come to sit heavily on rounded shoulders. The oppressor had taken everything, including that which produced the goodness, till all the goodness was gone. It was surely time to go.

Within the being of resigned men, there may arise a spark to move their thoughts and actions to greater aspirations, to better and easier lives. No-one knows how these sparks ignite and, indeed, for many, they never do and so a short and sad ending follows. For the spark-holders there is often a time of greater conflict and hardship and many give up. For the few who don't give up there is no certainty of anything – they walk the knife edge between belief and uncertainty, believing they are walking towards some kind of betterment but wondering if and how they will achieve it.

And so the theft of a boat is suggested and it happens – no analysis, no pondering, no real discussion or preparation. It seems like a good idea and it is done – a bag of food and clothes is packed and the six

gather at the water's edge on a moonless night. A particular boat is
suggested and none disagree – they simply push it into the water and
quietly row from the shore.

These empty-eyed men with frozen hearts and stealthy strides well
knew the stories of the sinkings and drownings. They'd even seen one
empty and broken boat returned, spat out by an ungrateful sea.

But when your head's in the gutter, held down by a savage English
boot, you've nothing to hope for but in the whims of your silent, unfor-
giving God. Even hope in the most gutless God was more to be reached
for than in their daily despair and starving kin. They well knew their
wives and bairns would suffer and wail when they learned their men
had departed but the men reasoned – if desperate and famished men
can be said to reason – their illicit flight in the sodden night would
bring unimagined riches and regular food in some unimaginable future. Their families would eventually be grateful.

They well knew the bastard English would not welcome them across
the Irish Sea but they'd heard stories of sufferless lives and smiling
faces. Unimaginable! Though their heads may be trampled, yet again,
into the gutters, they'd at least be gutters lined with gold and promise.
They only had to pass through the icy grip of this wild and wilful sea,
bear whatever indignities the blasted English would toss at them and
keep hope alive in hearts that died at each morning's awakening.

Any one of them could have slipped, hurt themselves or accidentally made a noise but, somehow, they were quick and silent, as they
needed to be. Their desperation lent them stealth and on their wings of
panic they flew. They upturned the boat, carried it to the water, climbed
in and were rowing from the shore before any of them had a moment to
reflect on their actions. As one creature, with six warming bodies, they
bent to the one thing that took them from fear to relief – being as far
from the shore as soon as possible.

Only after they realised they had accomplished their first objective
– off the land of their dreadful lives – did their animal instincts of flight
relax and their human thoughts intrude.

As their oars dipped near-silently into the water, the boat rocked
awkwardly. They kept rowing and quickly developed a rhythm as will
pendulum clocks in the same room. The panic of getting away, of being
spotted or heard, and of being returned to a worse peril than they had
lived to date slowly gave rise, with each oar-stroke, to an excitement

and realization that their months of dreaming had come to fruition. As the possibility of real freedom – so different from imagined freedom – grew, minds relaxed a little, though the sea did not. Though oars kept plying the water, now rising against them, with quiet strength, the focus of minds was able to move from what needed to be done, second by second, to what had been done and the consequences of that. Our minds move our bodies and so the white-knuckle grip on oars relaxed slightly.

One of the men, Sean, thought of a poignant moment of home and touched the rough fabric slung over his shoulder, and the crude pocket in which his special charm was kept. As his hand swept up from and back to oar, for reassurance, the wooden piece flew out of the pocket.

"Oh, hell!" he said in a loud whisper and immediately regretted his outburst. He imagined his voice carrying itself quickly across the flat water to the fat guard, snoring in his box, above the upturned boats. His exclamation would waken the guard who would sit up and waddle out with a lighted taper and discover the boat missing. Their flight to safety would be over before it had begun, all because of his impulsive outburst.

His friend beside him, Keryn, quickly patted his shoulder and Sean's eyes, now used to the darkness, saw Keryn's gentle smile. "Don't worry, my friend," Keryn was saying with his silent nod. "Just keep rowing now."

Slightly reassured, Sean focused his body more on keeping power and rhythm to his oar-stroke. He could not, however, keep his mind off the possibility of his precious talisman falling into the water. It had taken him a long while to find such a piece of wood and it had taken him longer to find a stone sharp enough to carve – to hack, really, if he was honest – a shape that pleased him. He had no idea why it was so important that he fashion his own keepsake – maybe it just helped to take his mind off the pain and drudgery of a life he'd been cast into. Whatever the reason, he had carried the piece of wood and chipping stone for over a year and, when he was happy with the shape, his wooden friend for yet another year.

Even in the worst of times, in the worst of lives, there lives the creative spark, that desire to create something meaningful. His spark had never gone out and it may have been that which kept him going till now. God knows, there were plenty of people he knew who had not made it. While so many others he toiled with had died of starvation, disease and injuries, he'd survived – hopeful day by hopeful day. And that hope, that dream of freedom had got him to this – the rising of water as boat and oars coursed their way to his and his friends' freedom. Such fervent hope and imagination must, eventually, give rise to opportunities in line with that hope and imagination. And only the stoutest soul then says, "Yes!" to the opportunity and does something about it. They all had and they were happy.

Though these six men were thin, weakened by starvation, they bore their pain with stoicism. Sean knew he had to give up on his beloved carved wood and his muscles plied the oars while his mind floated in the turbulent sea, searching forlornly for what would never be found.

They bent to the oars, the exertion warming them and the now-lashing sea chilling them. They took turns to rest, to eat a little and then return to their labours, desperation and hope lending power to flagging muscles.

Though without timepieces, they knew by the rising sun that their flight had been close to fifteen hours.

Keryn's call of sight of land, through the mist, was dismissed as fancy. It was too much to hope for but so much hoped for. All six oars relaxed as the men turned to see what Keryn had. They smiled and bent their heads, tears rising to blood-shot eyes. So close!

"Come on, lads!" commanded Sean, knowing he must not allow them to fall at the last ditch. "Our future's in sight. Let's collect on it."

They nodded as one creature and dug into the water as never before. The rugged craft rose to the call and soared into and over the welcoming waves. Surfing in, they beached on a pebble shore, leapt from the boat and caressed the stones. The stones were no different from Irish ones and, looking up, Sean saw that the grey English sky was identical to the grey Irish one. He wondered if the flight and pain had been worth it … then his eye spied a branch as it was flung to the pebbles. No, not a branch, it was carved by more than nature's buffeting. It was carved by man. He rose and stumbled back to the water's edge to pick up his sacred, lost talisman.

What could a man do but hug it to his heart and believe, beyond the evidence before him, that life was now on the turn – a sufferless life and smiling faces were his to claim, at last.

The Old System

There was a time, not so long ago, that the people of our village had a different system for making themselves and other things better. Looking back on this time of past days, it is hard to imagine that the old system actually worked and one might even think that it made life very, very hard, and even unbearable for some. We must remember, Dear Friend, that we are now living in a different time and have become used to a new system. Our time is our time and is all we know - it is really quite difficult to see how any other system (apart from ours) would work. But, from our now perspective, I will try to explain the old system and maybe we can see some benefits in it, and some improvements we can make to our present system. I did not live in that time so please excuse me if I have got it all wrong - some of it seems strange, but I will try to tell it as it was told to me.

The main idea of the old system seemed to be that you got happiness or power or respect or whatever else you wanted, by taking it from someone else. It appears that what you did was to tell everyone what a bad person someone else was, so that you could take the position that person held. At the same time, that other person told one and all what a bad, useless, unreliable or whatever sort of person you were, to retain their position and to stop you from getting it. This system was not only used by the ordinary people, but was used by some very important and well respected people. This may be hard to believe but I was told that the leaders of the village, those whom all looked to for guidance and example, even used this system. I was once told that these were the very people who actually started and maintained the system, but that seems absurd - someone was probably just testing my gullibility.

If you were making something that you wanted others to enjoy, you made them pay for it - with bits of paper, I think. Then with these bits of paper you could pay for the things you wanted - more grapes, a house, cars, food, fun and so on.

There was an unlimited supply of these pieces of paper if they kept being moved around so no one needed to miss out, but a few could not believe in this limitlessness. They feared, for some reason unknown to them, that there might not be enough for them so they started hoarding these bits of paper. Then, as others saw these few holding on to their bits of paper, this fear of lack for themselves grew. Before they knew it, everyone was fearing their lack of bits of paper and other abundance and people began to store up and hold on to everything that could be stored and held on to - pieces of paper, property and even respect and love from others. All the while, their heart-knowing was that if all was kept circulating, there would always be abundance for all, but their mind-fear was stronger and overruled this inner knowing. This may seem sad to you, Dear Friend, sitting here today, but in that time there was no sadness. In fact, so it seems, they were very proud of their system and had many names for it - Competition, Capitalism, Communism, Laissez Faire, Market Economy, Rivalry, Darwinism - names we know nothing of in these times. There were many names as the system reached into every aspect of their lives - education, business, science, philosophy, politics, relationships, child-rearing - and culminated in something they called warfare, whatever that is.

In business you may have produced something (say, wine) for others to enjoy. So, you tried to get as many bits of paper for each bottle of wine as you could get, to amass much and be happy. If people didn't want to pay you so much for your wine you would then sell them something else they wanted. You might try to sell them some fun or health or sex-appeal or success or other thing they wanted. You still made wine and sold bottles of it but it was not wine any longer, but fun or health or whatever.

If people still did not want to pay so much for this wine (or fun) you might then get a prominent person like a sporting personality, politician, film or television star, to tell everyone how great your wine was. To choose the right person to do this, they had to be admired and famous and they should know very little about your product. The buyers would then not be buying wine or fun but the fame and success of that person. I think they called this advertising and it was supposed to save you using up more pieces of paper to make a better wine that people really wanted to buy. However, you had to give many bits of paper to the people who did this advertising for you, I am told. I am not really sure why it was done. Perhaps it was easier to sell instant success and fame than good wine.

Then again, you might have raised the price of your wine to get more bits of paper. If someone didn't want to pay that much they would criticise your wine and offer to pay less. You would retaliate by criticising their judgement and say it was very valuable wine. You might, then, have reduced the price a little and they may, grudgingly, have paid more than they wanted and after much haggling and criticism an unhappy deal would have been reached, with both parties telling themselves they had made a bargain.

Or, if it was inner things you wanted to store up, like self-esteem, you could criticise someone's personality or life-style to make yours seem better. One winner, one loser. Like the sport they used to have, there was always a winner and a loser and the balance was kept.

When my brother and I first heard about this system he, a rural type, said that it sounded like two dogs fighting. One might have bitten a piece off the other and swallowed that piece. He then took on more of the other dog's being (its strength and power) while the other dog lost it. Then the bigger and stronger dog could win easier and took bigger and bigger bites, until he was massive and the other dog diminished. That analogy seemed a bit harsh to me, though.

Now, Dear Friend, you may wonder how the old system changed to the new. It was a slow transition and started with one person.

One day, a stranger came to town and when the inn-keeper told him the price of the room he didn't argue or criticise, but accepted it with grateful thanks and mentioned what an attractive inn it was. The inn-keeper was stunned - he wasn't used to such talk and couldn't think what to say. Then, later, the stranger told him what a beautiful meal he had been served and how comfortable the room was. The inn-keeper could only stand open-mouthed - having compliments thrust at him was so unnerving. As the stranger prepared to leave, the inn-keeper found himself taking 20% off the bill. With the reduced cost, the stranger decided to stay a while longer and told the inn-keeper what a generous person he was. The really unnerving part of it was that the stranger seemed to sincerely mean what he said - he wasn't playing word-games and trying to trip him up, like others sometimes did.

"Queer sod", he thought. "You don't do business by talking about generosity." He did, however, start to warm to the stranger and his ways, which was something he hadn't done with anyone else before.

The news of this stranger and his weird ways soon spread and people began to stare and wonder. Some, knowing he was only a fake, would taunt and criticise him and would then be surprised when the stranger smiled back and said something nice. It sets a bloke back when someone won't reply in the customary way, particularly when he admires your new suit or car or something.

Some of the weaker-minded people would just smile at him. He would smile back and somehow a gentle conversation would develop - no arguing or criticisms, just talk of the weather and an interest in each other's thoughts and lives. It took some getting used to for most, but after a while many people found themselves emulating his behaviour at times.

In those days, it seems, their system of working together or politics (as they called it) was very different. I can't quite get my mind around it but it appears that a small group of people would boast publicly to the masses, about how nice they were and about lots of good things they would do for the people if they would let them be bosses. The people would then ask this small group to be their bosses - this seemed to happen every few years. When this happened, this small group would then call themselves politicians and decide for the people what was best for them, without actually considering the real needs of the people and with little regard for the things they had said when they wanted to become politicians. If these politicians wanted the people to do something for them that the people didn't want to do, they would create what they called laws and the people would have to obey. If they didn't obey, there were strong people who were given many bits of paper by the politicians to force their will, their laws, on the people. The politicians thought of all sorts of punishments that the strong people meted out on the disobedient people.

For some reason, the people accepted the laws and punishments and left it to the politicians to decide all things for them. This was a very onerous task for the politicians and the people gave the politicians many,

many bits of paper to run their lives for them. The system became so ingrained and accepted, that the people would only do what the laws demanded and they stopped thinking for themselves. This sounds very sad but they seemed very happy with that.

I tell you these things so you comprehend the import of what happened next.

This stranger was quite inquisitive and wanted to know all sorts of things about the peoples' lives. They were so pleased that someone was interested in them and told him more than he ever asked. It is hard to know what he thought for he kept his opinions to himself. He simply asked and listened. However, as these people had so many opinions about things but had never explained to anyone what they did or why they did things, they started wondering - questioning themselves and each other.

The more simple-minded ones seemed to do the most questioning and wondering. The more intelligent ones had all the answers and said things like "because it is the law" or "because the politicians said so". They were happy with that. The simple-mindeds, though, were not altogether happy and eventually started asking these same questions of the politicians. Most people had forgotten the nice words and promises the politician-hopefuls had said, but some didn't forget. They, in their simple ways, wanted to know about the nice words and why things weren't as promised.

Some of the politicians acted quite odd when this happened and they eventually made a law to stop people questioning. This was the first law that didn't work as it started more people questioning things. Someone told the strong people it was the fault of the stranger and they locked him away. When some broke in and freed stranger, everyone was confused.

The politicians started yelling at the people and saying nasty things about them. This was very confusing as the politicians had always been such nice people, looking after and helping everyone. The people didn't know whether the big task the politicians had was too big for them or not, and started wondering if there was another way to run their lives, to take the strain off the politicians. This made the politicians even madder and they made more laws and tougher punishments.

Meanwhile the stranger was getting confused at all the fuss made over him and the odd way the people were acting because he had asked some questions. This had never happened where he had come from, but he didn't say that. He just wondered a little more and smiled sadly.

It seems sad that before a new system can come in, the worst of the old one has a need to manifest itself. Another sadness is that when some people gain a measure of power, they feel an unstoppable urge to have more and more power. Then when this power-base is challenged they tend to make complete fools of themselves by taking absurd measures to retain that power - measures that actually ensure their own downfall.

The nice thing here, though, is that the New System was started by one simple man. He had no intention of creating change and couldn't have done it on his own, but without him it may not have happened. While we each cannot change the world, we can provide keys to change and then leave it to others to decide whether or not to turn the key and open the door to the new.

The result of all this wondering and questioning and the backlash of more laws (which created more questioning) was that many people realised that they were able to make their own decisions. This was probably easier for the simple-minded people who could not analyse consequences and just did what was right for their heart-knowing. For those of higher intelligence it became a very fearful time for they now had to take responsibility for their actions and had no person or laws to fall back on. But, as they say, time and tide waits for no man, and no matter how many were locked away and punished, the CHANGE was upon the village and no one could turn it back. In spite of the increasing yelling and punishments, the CHANGE quietly asserted itself. The politicians and strong people found themselves either quietly changing within or moving to another village where the Old System was stronger.

The people then realised that they were without leaders and, not being used to this, desperately looked around for some. The stranger was the obvious choice but he initially refused, not wanting to exert his will over others. He then realised that this time of CHANGE was very fearsome for many and he agreed to lead for a time. Although he was a very simple man, he was also very clever (or are simplicity and cleverness the same?) and only pretended to lead. He would ask the people what they wanted and then he would say, "O.K., that is the law". His laws were very easy to change and get rid of and gradually there became very few laws.

Under the Old System they felt that there had to be laws to keep control, for if the people did what they wanted there would be bedlam. But the stranger showed the people (without actually telling them) that if they each did what their inner heart-knowing told them, then it worked perfectly with what everyone else wanted to do.

Although most of the bits of paper were taken by those who left for other villages, there still seemed to be many bits of paper around. I am not sure what happened to the advertising people but that activity ceased, for people just knew what was good and right for them. The wine and other products miraculously improved and people really enjoyed making the best that they could. The bits of paper disappeared later to be replaced by our simpler system of exchange.

The stranger actually created a leadership which made him redundant, which pleased him mightily, bringing us to the situation we now have where the only leader is the hearts of the people.

We have had our system for some time now but, as you know, the only constant is change and I feel that a new CHANGE is upon us. Thankfully, we learn from the past and any new CHANGE will be even better than we now have. There is a new man in the village who seems very wise and wants to create an agreement where all bottles of wine are sold at the same price and all workers get the same reward for their work. This sounds more equitable than this system where all these things are agreed between parties and are not always the same. And so we move, yet again, into a new and totally different way from any other system before. In time we will probably look back and not be able to understand why we had the system we have now.

Changes

There was a time, a time yet to be, when things were different. This time is seen with such clarity and closeness that it is a wonder it is not here now. Its inevitability is astounding and already many see it as if it is the present. For those people who have yet to pull the thin veil aside, we tell of this future time.

The differences we tell of are many; so many that we, having lived in both times, still cannot imagine them all. We cannot remember every change and you cannot be expected to imagine a tiny fraction of them. To say that the movement from your now to our then was traumatic is a gross understatement, but to imagine thunderbolts, catastrophe, wars, pain and sadness is to misunderstand the nature of these changes. There were certainly thunderbolts, catastrophe, wars, pain and sadness, and they were there for those who still held to the old belief that change is always accompanied by pain and suffering. Many others also needed drama in their lives and so that was provided for them too, as always.

However, for those of you who know that changes can be beautiful and joyful, your changes happened with such gentleness and acceptance, it is a wonder we still marvel over. So do not be afraid of them for your joy in them will create something beyond what you could have imagined. Those changes are happening while you read these words and it may not be until a later time that you recognise the reality of them, both within and without.

The story of these changes is written within your heart and within the heart of every Earthly being. All people, animals, plants, rocks and even Mother Earth herself, have a heart. Every heart responded to the heart-call - a call that linked every heart as one. The oneness of hearts is the core of the changes that occurred and within that oneness came the true aliveness of all individuals, the realisation of the full glory of our essence and beauty. The combining and linking of all of these great souls gave rise to an Earth of such tremendous beauty and joy, that we still, oftentimes, shed a tear for the love with which we were blessed. Please do not deny your potential or that you deserve such love and joy. Our sadness is that we believe in your deservedness more than you do. When your self-love was heightened, your love of all others rose, allowing these beautiful changes to manifest without any physical action necessary on your part. You did, however, find yourself compelled by that self-love to extend that love to others in some tangible way. That action further accelerated your self-love and boundless joy.

If you stand beside the river you may see it as a turbulent, frothing torrent. However, if you dip your toe into the calm eddy at the edge you will see the turbulence quieten and by the time you have lowered your whole body into that warm and inviting water, the river has become a smoothly gliding golden stream of love. If you can but relax and allow, you will recall a forgotten ability to float and accept the flow - wherever it takes you. There may be rocks in the stream, but as you connect to their heart and release your fear of them, you will find the stream guides you around them with such gentleness, you wonder why you held onto those fears for so long.

This gentle flowing is the way you moved into the Age of Heart, the Age of Oneness. Love replaced fear and all realised that they were part of the all. You became the stream, the rocks and more of yourself and as you realised the love within, you asked "How can there be any fear?" In that warm and golden stream was every other self-loving being, going in the same direction, gently touching hearts and helping each other to stay afloat and to flow.

For you to understand your future as it happened we will take you back to your past, to see the process that led to your now.

There have been many shifts and waves that have changed the consciousness and actions of people. You will know from your history books and from your own inner knowing that the Renaissance was a large leap in the consciousness of art and culture. You will know that the industrial revolution changed life forever in rural England and the rest of the world.

You then saw the breakdown of the archetypal religion and a vacuum occurred and a cynical atheistic consciousness pervaded where people were saying "I will just grab what I can. I'll grab this sex, I'll grab that money and I'll use up the world as soon as I can because I've got no God to answer to. I've got no spiritual responsibility."

This epitomised itself in communism and in Russia was the biggest rape of the planet - it had more nuclear waste and more irreverence to nature than any other culture. It was the culture of materialism. Thus it was an atheistic culture which kicked out the church and replaced it with an absolute arrogance of ego.

So then you discovered a new spirituality, but not a spirituality with a personal God like a big daddy in the sky, or a Santa coming down the chimney. It was a spirituality that your children may have been teaching you at this time. Perhaps you listened to them and heard their wisdom.

This new spirituality was learning about the intelligence of nature - cellular intelligence. The cell multiplies in the womb in the same way as a tree or a sparrow and they all have the same cellular intelligence, as have the oceans and the mountains. That intelligence is sensitive and if you interfere with that intelligence it will destroy you, as well as itself. So the new God that united humanity was the Earth Spirit and the balance of the cosmos - "don't junk space".

The new religion was not a fancy religion like a great communication with the Masters, but a simple communication with the cellular intelligence of all living things. The new spirituality was this understanding that you had to respect and honour the intelligence of the Earth through understanding its intelligence. From that everyone became united. Every religion had a bit of it but the need was to be united with the cellular universe and the magical building blocks of life - D.N.A.

You realised that with this new religion, or spirituality, there need be no gurus or priests or 'higher' beings telling you what to believe in or what to think. You were the guru, the wise elder and the best teacher you could imagine, for you could link directly with the God source, through the tangible and natural things around you. From nature (which does not discriminate, judge or segregate) you realised the unity of your world and the allness of the universe. As an oak tree will not stop grass growing around it, you found that it was not necessary to put up any boundaries or territorial defences. As the marsh plants find the swamps, and the pohutukawas grow at the edges of the sea, you found the places that best suited your particular needs and your natural rhythms. All were free to find their power spots and the boundaries between territories and beliefs simply dissolved.

Instead of dumping thousands of tonnes of corn in the Pacific to keep the price up, that corn was shared among those who were starving. Instead of "Cold Wars" where nations did not speak, leaders actively encouraged the communion and sharing of economic and technological progress. The white people of the world went to the darker skinned races to learn of their ancient wisdom and a greater sharing began to take place. This gave rise to the realisation of the universal truth, contained in all religions and beliefs. For example, it was found that the Maori, Maya and Tibetan calendars were the same and this and thousands of other similarities brought the realisation that we are all one, and people started to wonder why the boundaries and borders had ever been put up. As the Chinese say, "The only enemy you have is the man you have not met".

The plastic age, which started with bakelite, grew to a stage where everything was made from plastic - shoes, aircraft, ships and even homes. Mankind had found a substance that was a derivative of nature, but it could never replace, hygienically and harmoniously, the other substances of nature. He tried to overrule wood and other natural substances, which caused a revolution called the Hippie Generation which revolted against this very plastic consciousness, this artificiality.

China, once great, had declined into a materialistic, non-respectful and decaying nation with a dictatorship and a brainwashed populace. This country, the last vestige of materialism, had to succumb to the new spirituality. It did not do it willingly so there had to be a war. There was no way China could win as the west had far superior technology - technology cannibalised from crashed extraterrestrial craft. A month after the stealth bomber was built, it was obsolete. In Bosnia, the United States used the neutron bombs which killed people but left property undamaged. China could not match this technology and had to succumb. For a time, the United States was reluctant to use this technology for world peace, but the leaders of the country, the financiers, had to finally listen to the mass mind crying out for peace. This mass mind of connected and cooperating peace seekers was even stronger than the flower children of the Hippie Generation. This strength and crying was not, though, of a violent mind. The gentle flowering of a peace consciousness simply touched people's minds and they flowed with it.

By the 1980's this artificiality had reached its zenith. Plastic came with the computer age, the age of greed and the age of superficiality - the YUPPIE Generation, worldwide. All of a sudden there was a counter-move and the Age of Naturalism began. People began saying that science must blend with the indigenous nature of the soul. The bureaucrat, the politician and every person in society began to get in touch with their natural selves, the indigenous being, the Earth Man. They started to make healthier houses with wooden floors, woollen rugs and earth walls, as had been made by the Pueblos, the Egyptians and countless other civilisations for centuries before. This natural technology harmonised with nature, and history turned unexpectedly against the predictions of science fiction writers who had seen an advancing plastic technological age.

So, obviously, in this age of naturalism, everyone was trying to get back in touch with Earth and their indigenous selves. Of course, everybody was indigenous and everyone was a conqueror. Some of the "conquered" people were saying that their conquerors were unfair and they wanted their land back. But people realised that it was like a 20th century man saying the Normans conquered his ancestors and he wanted his land back, with the unconscious knowing that he had Norman blood in his veins and so he didn't have a case. So, for example, a Maori going to court to get land back from the white man didn't have a case as he had white blood in him. There were, of course, legitimate needs for different people to be acknowledged and given a fair go in society but it was seen as ridiculous when one race developed an attitude of being superior, in a territory.

The Age of Naturalism meant that people had to get the right teaching so that they could really advance that mega trend of knowledge, to understand the power of the Earth and the grid system. Even a moron knew that in walking in the Andes, it felt different. Even a moron knew that Stonehenge had a special power. Every living being came to understand that the Earth is a living being - that it has pulse centres, dark areas and dead centres - that the erupting volcanoes are just like human skin when it gets toxic and blasts forth in a seething boil and cleans itself. It was, and is, a normal process for a body that is in disease, and the Earth was in disease. It was in trouble and had to blast forth.

One way Earth was helped in its healing process was by stopping the exploitation of the forests and the destruction of its nerves. People realised that if they wiped out all of the forests, they cut away the protection and exposed the skin to infection, and common sense prevailed.

The move to the Natural Age meant that your technology changed radically. The move went from being empathetic with nature, to working alongside nature and then to working from nature herself. This meant that your plastic, combustion, electric and electronic technologies became obsolete. (We can feel our scribe quaking over this thought as he loves his computer, stereo, car and motorbike. But he need not be afraid.) The natural technology was discovered and phased in gently, as a feather landing in your hand. You were not thrown into a time warp of cave-man times and left with no technology at all, as some of your seers predicted.

So, you may ask, are cars and computers of the future to be made of mud and grass? Well, yes, sort of ... In time you discovered that it was possible to grow anything you like, as you do with your plants now. The system grew to be more developed than that though.

One way was to create a liquid and then set, within it, an archetypal or electrified grid of the machine you wanted. Your machine - a computer, toaster, spacecraft or whatever - would then grow, as crystals do, only quicker. When you entered your spacecraft you would see that the controls were organic and, as such, very flexible. As you travelled to other places with different frequencies you could change the molecular structure of the craft and could simply teleport or dissolve to become one with the new environment. If you took on passengers you could make it grow larger to accommodate them.

With your computer you could grow it to your original archetypal grid and then, as your requirements changed, you could change the structure, shape and size of your machine.

It was a time of great magic and learning but, as always, it was a two-edged sword. As you were working with nature, you had to be totally in harmony with her. You learned the best time to do certain things with the phases of the moon, the rotation of the sun and many other natural cycles. Just as many civilisations had found over the centuries preceding your time, particularly in Europe, if trees are chopped down at a certain time (2 particular days every 4 years) then the wood does not burn or rot - perfect for house building. So you found the best time and method for working with and altering these organic machines. It was also found that as nature was sensitive, these machines mysteriously refused to function if your intent in using them was evil. They were powered by love.

As the abundance of the Earth was being depleted by human over-population, the Natural Man could not help but adapt to that and the female cycle changed from a lunar rhythm to a solar one and synchronised with the other creatures and the seasons and they became fertile at only one time of the year. It created more space for all other creatures - the ones you have now and many other wondrous ones that appeared. Man benefited from this in more ways than you can imagine.

Because humans were more in tune with nature and themselves, lie detectors became obsolete. It also meant that offenders were treated differently. In your present system, a battered wife who defends herself and accidentally kills her aggressor is treated the same as a vicious, intentional murderer who does it for the kicks. You, later, were able to see the heart and intentions of people and, in these cases, the woman would be given love and support while the murderer would be put to sleep, allowing the world of spirit to deal with him. That woman was not a danger to society but the murderer was. Locking people away was seen to serve no purpose and the millions spent on prisons went to children and others in need.

Your friend, Jesus, said that the meek shall inherit the Earth. This was close to the truth and, as humans realised they were the children of the Earth, the Earth inherited the meek, and was mightily pleased.

The Builder Boy

In silence we tell our real story.

He would pick up the sticks, one by one, and carefully place them on the pile. He would lay them next to each other, ten one way and then the next layer of ten at right-angles, slowly building his creation with no intention but to see it take its shape. The sticks were just broken twigs or branches, roughly formed as nature had designed. From these irregular creations would evolve his own creation of symmetry. Time would flow by without his consciousness of it, as his beautiful little building grew. Then a time would come when he had had enough – it was completed and he would walk away with a contented feeling of completion.

Sometimes his little buildings would remain undisturbed for days, till the wind, birds or people scattered them. He had created, and what happened after that mattered not – the form would be moved to another state by other forces. Sometimes, his older brother would become exasperated by these silly piles of sticks and kick them over. This might happen while he was building or it might happen later. He was puzzled by his brother's brutish actions – he simply wondered why the sight of his simple pile could evoke so much anger.

His brother thought, "What a waste of time" and, "What pointless and useless things they were". The piles of sticks were a silly waste of time and were so useless they would be scattered by his violent feet. There was sadness for this angry brother and, some time later, the younger boy would start another pile with an inner smile of contentment. He knew his piles had no relevance or use but the building of them gave him peace.

As his first mind chose sticks and placed them, his second mind would go wandering and wondering. In this second mind he would wonder why his brother got so angry and why a simple pile of sticks had so much control over him. As his first mind became more focused on an intricate and beautiful creation, his second mind would be more free to soar to new understandings. He would try to understand how his brother thought and felt, and why. Once in a while, for a fraction of a second, he would become his brother and would understand a little more. Then, at other times, less frequently, he would receive a flash of knowing, an insight, an answer. Whether these flashes came from a third mind or some other place, he didn't know and didn't really care. What he did know was that, in a random sort of way, his questions were being answered.

In time, he realised that his own world was one of means and his brother lived in a world of ends. Some people might say that "the ends justify the means" while others saw no ends – there were only means. Thus the world was divided in two. Thus there was misunderstanding. Thus did people hurt other people. Thus were laws needed.

The boy's brother had a need of ends, of tangible results, of completion and acclamation for those results. Because these ends needed limited resources (people's time, thought and assets) to produce, any creation that did not use these resources productively, took from those that could be productive, useful and acclaimed.

As he became an ends person, in those split seconds that he was his older brother, he felt a tightening of some sort of restriction and he called it fear, at first. This was not a pleasant sensation but he felt a need to understand it, for it was something he had never experienced before. As his first mind built another pile of sticks, his second called in that restricting feeling and, in his wondering, he went into the fear and, in the dim light of that fear, he saw a smallness he had never known. It puzzled him. A much smaller world appeared before him and he felt an apprehension and wondered at it. As this new sensation grew, he felt a sense of urgency, as if there was limited time and he had to do something. What he had to do, he didn't know, but action was needed – any action. It was as if he didn't do something, anything, he would lose something. He felt a need to create or acquire something, anything. In this small world in which he found himself, there were so few things and his urge was to produce and acquire – almost as if he didn't, he would lose the little he already had and so would the rest of the world.

And, in this strange little world, everything seemed to be so untidy – there was no pattern and his urge was to rearrange it and to tidy it. If it wasn't tidied, it would become untidier, and, in its untidiness, would fall apart and could very well destroy itself. He was needed to save it from its imminent self-destruction. It was up to him as everyone else seemed bent on making it more untidy, more likely to self-destruct. The feeling was one of quiet desperation and there was no one else to help him in this task.

And, as he searched around for others to help with this mammoth task, he realised that no one cared and that no one was at all concerned with the mess, the untidiness and the imminent danger. Everyone was in their own little world, making things worse and he was it – the only one who could save the world from its inevitable fate. He felt very alone, separate and unable to cope with all that needed to be done. And yet, it just had to be done and he seemed to be the only person who was able and willing to do it.

As the boy eased out of his second mind, he felt quite weak and stopped his building. He stopped everything and just sat, panting a little and very confused. If this was the world of his brother, it was not a nice place to be. As he sat, with both minds in neutral, there grew an unnerving feeling of disconnection within him – an odd feeling that he was separate from his body, the ground, trees, sky, birds, people and all other things. And, as this feeling of separateness grew, he felt a growing pain in his stomach, a great pain of loneliness and fear. The birds, trees, grass and other things that had been his friends, all seemed very distant and alien – almost as if they had become enemies. Instead of being able to talk to them, as he had in the past, they now spoke in a language he didn't understand. In each second, his loneliness, fear and pain grew and he felt an overwhelming desire to lash out at a world that seemed to be laughing at him.

Just then, his brother came by and angrily kicked over the small pile of twigs yet again. He was very surprised when the younger boy leapt up, screamed and punched him to the ground. The fury was so savage that the older brother had a forehead scar for the rest of his life.

The younger boy built no more. His fear and anger grew as he lost sight of the secret world that he had always communed with. His anger fuelled a need to compete, to be better than everyone and to reshape an untidy world. He excelled in sport and became a successful, if ruthless, politician. The more he forced the world into a shape of his own, the more distance he felt from it – this fuelled his anger even more and so he pushed harder, competed more and felt more alone.

This spiral kept turning downwards until, one day, after a heart-attack, divorce and election defeat (all in six months), he crashed. He sat in his lonely apartment and did nothing, except cry. For the first time in all of his forty years, the tears were allowed out and he ached, sobbed and sat. In the stillness he saw the desperation, anger and fear that had controlled him and the sobbing would erupt from his heaving chest in painful bursts. But, try as he might, he couldn't move from that stillness. It enveloped him and he could do no more than sit and cry in lonely pain.

Eventually, he gave up fighting the iron grip of that aching stillness. As he gave in, the grip was released, the pain eased and he cried the sweet tears of relief. Released from the stillness by his forgiving, he grew to like it and he would relax in it for hours, eyes closed, enjoying the nothingness. And, in that nothingness, the childhood connection with all things returned and his loneliness eased. The oneness of himself and of his world grew and, with it, came back a strength and peace he hadn't known since his youthful building days.

As the weeks went by, he would venture into the public places and, as he sat, people would be drawn to him and would tell him of their pains, sorrows and regrets. He would simply listen, smile and allow them to pass on, happier. Soon, larger groups would gather and they'd ask him about things, somehow feeling he knew the answers. Seldom did he have any answers, but his questions prompted their self-discovery. Then he'd be asked to speak to groups and, though he felt he had nothing to say, words would come to soothe the listeners. Then they'd ask for more and he'd answer them in his silence and they'd go away happier.

Though he sought it not, he became a builder of people and a re-builder of their lives and memories. It actually seemed so simple to him, but he was constantly honoured for his wisdom, healing words and quiet ways.

And, every once in a while, he'd pick up a pile of sticks and build

     51 Moments With Fables

a little creation. Nobody kicked them over now. People would watch and copy and, eventually, they built stick creations to symbolize the religion they created around him. And he felt sad for them ...

Lessons From A Washing Machine

Sitting here waiting for the washing-machine to finish, I keep thinking that it must stop soon. I listen and it hums, so it must be going. I carry on reading and, again, wonder if it is finished yet. Still humming, still going. I do something else and then listen again - still humming. Finally, intrigued, I go and check with my eyes and its lights are on …. Then I realise that I had forgotten to turn the taps on. It was wanting to go but I had held it back through a simple oversight. I turn the taps on and the humming turns to action.

How often does this happen in life? We want to be someone, to do something and it remains an elusive far-off dream. Whatever we do, however hard we try, the dream remains just that - a dream. Stubbornly we keep chasing it, pushing, doing, wanting …. and never achieving. So we get determined and work harder, push harder, dream harder but that crazy dream stays just beyond arm's length. We feel cheated and it seems we have gone backward, not forwards. All the money, time and energy has been wasted.

Then, we think, there are two choices. One is to give up but we know if we follow that one, that darned dream will dog us forever. A forever "I wish I had done that" feeling will plague us for the rest of our days.

The second is to get angry, determined and downright stubborn about it. If we force a little harder, then something has to give. So we waste more money, time, energy and friendships and that stupid goal stands just far enough away to safely jeer at us.

If, at those times, I had got off my bottom, out of my way and looked at myself (and my goal) as dispassionately and as simply as I had looked at the washing-machine, then the answers (and the dream) would have simply flooded in - as the water did when I turned on the taps.

Usually, the answers are so simple that we kick ourselves for not seeing them sooner. We are looking so hard at the tough and complicated choices, that the easy little ones are overlooked.

Sometimes we feel that we want to progress but 'life' or our friends or our money or the universe is holding us back. Then we stop, step back (sometimes!) and look ever so dispassionately at ourselves and our situation and we realise that everything was gunning for us - opportunities, friends, universe, ourselves - but there was some silly little thing we forgot, like undoing the seat-belt before we got out of the car or moving the car before slamming down the garage door.

I suppose that some people don't ever stop to listen to that little voice that tells them their tie is sticking out of their fly or their skirt is tucked into their knickers. They keep pushing and doing and as the road gets rougher and narrower they go faster, and die in some untimely way. Illness and disaster are only Nature's way of telling us "You are doing it all wrong, Mate. Stop and rethink". Or perhaps it is Nature's way of saying "Stop thinking, and listen." Whatever the message or the problem, many don't know how to stop and listen - or perhaps they are too scared to. And so the problems mount and, for some, death is the only way their own good sense can get them to stop and listen. It seems to work ....

Thankfully, for most of us, we do listen before that rather final stage. But when we do, we always wonder why we didn't stop ages ago. "Next time," we say, "I will listen to the little things and take heed." And as we are saying this to ourselves, we walk into the door or drive into a ditch.

Then we wonder what it is that we are doing wrong. So often it is not what we are doing but that we are doing. Doing nothing, sometimes, can be very productive. For a start, it is easier on the door or the car. It also means that we can hear that little voice inside. And if we stop for long enough we can actually hear what that voice is saying. With practice we can have long, complicated conversations. With more practice, we can have very simple conversations and the answers that come through usually have us saying "Why didn't I think of that before, it's so simple?" or some such thing.

But, with the washing-machine, I had to expend energy, get off my backside and go and look. It takes energy to stop and look. When life is humming along and we are going for it, it takes energy to keep going. But, unlikely though it sounds, it takes more energy to stop and to listen. "How so?" you might ask. It can be summed up in four letters - FEAR. To stop, listen and revaluate takes courage. It takes a brave soul to look honestly within and say "Oops, I made a mistake. I'll now do it a different way." Far easier to save face and blunder on with a string of excuses and tomorrows. Stepping through that fear takes a lot of energy, a lot of courage. So we put it off as moving takes less energy than stopping.

But the silly thing is that if we expend the energy and take the courage to stop and listen, it is never as bad as we imagined. In fact, often it is fun. So what is this fear we have to step through? It is made up from the words False Energy Appearing Real, and once we face it we see its unreality and it vanishes.

So what have I learned here? I have learned that washing-machines make excellent teachers. Anything else? No, not really, for I have probably been too busy writing to listen. Perhaps it is time to stop ...

McDonalds Haircuts and Laundromat Dinners

Would you consider going to a chemist shop (drug store) to buy a car? If you wanted some deodorant, would you look for it at a car dealership? Silly questions? Don't be surprised if, in, say, three years' time, these are not silly questions but very normal ones.

When we want to exchange money in New Zealand, we go to a bank for that's where we get the best rate. However, because the banks in England are so greedy, they're the worst places to exchange your money. If we're going for a holiday to, say, Crete, we buy our euros at Marks & Spence, which is not a bank but best known as a supermarket and clothing store.

My wife, Anna, needed a new computer yesterday and, initially, we did the logical thing and went to Curries, England's largest retailer of computers. Their best deal was around £420. We went to Argos which is a general warehouse selling all manner of household goods and their best price was £399. Then we ended up on my computer, ordering hers over the internet from Tescos - originally a food supermarket - and got the same computer for £299 … plus a rebate … plus Clubcard points … plus free delivery!

So, if someone tells you they're getting their hair cut at McDonalds or are dining out at the local laundromat, it may not be their dementia kicking in but the new way of shopping … getting what you want from the most unlikely place imaginable ... a bit like my hero finding finance companies at the temple, 2,000 years ago!

A Body Of Questions

The boy often woke up with strange questions and ideas running through his head. No matter how many times it happened they still surprised him as they seemed to come from nowhere. They weren't the kind of things he learned at school or from his parents and friends. They were just there and no matter how hard he tried he couldn't get them to go away.

This morning it happened again and his brain was asking him why people were built like they were - you know, with feet at the bottom, head at the top, arms in the middle and all of that. Why weren't our ears lower down so people couldn't pull them? Why weren't our eyes somewhere else where dust and salt-water didn't get in? Why wasn't our stomach higher so the food didn't have so far to go? Such silly questions but whatever he did they wouldn't go away. He tried to redesign his body, in his mind, but he couldn't think of a better design.

He knew he had to work it out somehow so he asked his father at breakfast.

"Humph, you and your silly questions!" was the answer there.

He asked his mother and was told "Because that's the way we are. If we were different we wouldn't be humans."

It worried him that adults were happy not knowing the reasons for things. He loved learning things and didn't want to grow up if it meant his curiosity and learning for things would stop. There was so much to learn and he knew he couldn't do it all while he was a child.

He asked his friends on the way to school but they just giggled, looked at him strangely and continued talking about the latest Sega games and Michael Jackson.

"Michael Jackson!" he suddenly thought. "He's always experimenting with his body and changing things. Perhaps he'll know. I should write to him and ask. I'm sure he'll know."

But he needed to know right now and asked his teacher at lunch break. She smiled, listened and said, "I really don't know, but let's make a class project of it and see what ideas the others have."

When the teacher introduced the idea to the afternoon class no one giggled or looked strangely at her - they all got really interested and had a lot of fun thinking up ideas like: If your eyes were lower down they'd be covered by your clothes and you wouldn't see. And your stomach had to be lower down by your bottom so the food could get out easily. And if your mouth was on your stomach you'd have to get undressed to eat and nobody would hear what you were saying. Then they tried to redesign their bodies and some really funny drawings were made. But every time another idea was thought of someone would say why it wasn't a good idea. Then someone asked why there were only one each of the things in the middle - like nose, mouth and penis - and two of the things on the side - like eyes, arms, nipples and legs. Someone else said that if you only had one eye, arm and leg on one side you would flop over to one side, and things had to be balanced. They had a lot of fun with this project and some really funny and strange ideas and drawings were made. But, in the end, they decided that whoever designed the people's bodies must have been very clever because they couldn't think of one improvement.

After that the boy felt much better as everyone thought his questions were neat ones and he didn't feel so strange, after all.

On his way home from school, while he was kicking stones and watching the dust rising, he felt happier as many of his questions had been answered, but there was just one silly question in his mind - it didn't really matter where all your head-things were so why couldn't you have a big ear on your chin, one eye in the middle, two noses on the side and a mouth at the top? He leaned on a picket fence and dreamed up all sorts of head designs and wondered some more. Then he jumped as he heard a voice, very close.

"I see you be deep in toughts," said an old white-whiskered man, smiling. "I'm sorry to startle you but do you want to tell of dese toughts?" he asked.

The old man spoke strangely but had a happy twinkle in his eyes and looked really kind.

"You'll just think I'm silly," said the boy.

"Aha!" laughed the old man. "I think we's all pretty silly at times, me lad. And I sees dat da sillier you are, the cleverer you be. I be pretty silly but I grow da best vegetables 'round 'ere."

The old man's brown and wrinkled hand patted the boys little hand and the boy felt very peaceful.

"Aah … well," said the boy shyly. "I don't know where to start."

"Just startin' at one end and goin' trough to de odder end seems a good idea at times," smiled the old man.

The boy smiled at his funny way of talking and then told him of his day and his strange questions.

"Pretty deep stuff from one so young," smiled the old man. "I always be tinkin' strange toughts like that meself and it's a funny ting. Oftimes de answers come from the same place as do de questions - just from nowhere."

The boy brightened up. "So you know the answers, Sir? Can you please tell me now?"

"Ah, the impetuosity of youth! Always wantin' to know everyting now!" the old man chuckled, sort of to himself. "But don't be stoppin' the questions, laddie, for widout de questions there be no answers and you larn nuttin'."

The boy smiled, a little relieved that an adult (and a really old one) was still curious about things. "So why are we all built like we are?" asked the boy, in keen anticipation.

"Well, I'm not sure's I got de right answers coz I've never been to one of yar schools. I don't have no proper larnin' like y'all do," said the old man with a sigh. "I never went to school - just got shanghied on to a ship, at gun-point, at 14 and worked them square-riggers for many a year. Den in South Africa I fought dem Boers and den de Zulus. Den I skipped to 'Stralia to find gold dat wasn't there and den to India and ended up runnin' a tea plantat'n. That's where I learn'd 'bout growin' tings. The owner's wife wanted me to larn 'bout dem words and numbers. I still 'member most of dem too," he said proudly.

"Yes?," said the boy expectantly, wondering if he would ever get to the answer. He also wanted to know about the old man's adventures and tried to be patient.

"Well, I'm jest warnin' ya laddie," said the old man, seriously. "Me answers don't come from no 'telligent school teacher or from reading big books. I jest pieced it togedder from me uneducated mind. I've probably got it all wrong."

The boy waited eagerly, not wanting to interrupt.

"Well I seen dem Zulus in Africa and dese Aborigines in 'Stralia what just walk along and den just disappear - like dey go invisible. Den dey just reappear behind you or somewhere else. Sure surprises da hell out of you! I couldna figure it out but den a friend tol' me 'bout dis scientist chap (Einsteiny I tink 'is name was) who told his mates that nothing really existed - dat everyting was just energy, vibratin' at different speeds. Da slower da vibration da harder a ting is. So the sky vibrates faster 'n a tree what vibrates faster 'n a rock, and on it goes. Well, most of 'is mates tought he was balmy but me simple mind kinda hooked into the idea … you're looking puzzled, laddie."

"Yea … well … I've never heard of any of this," said the boy, wondering what was coming next.

"Dey don't tell you 'bout dis in yar fancy schools?" the old man asked, amazed.

"Well, not yet anyway," said the boy.

"Perhaps you'll hear 'bout it next week den," mused the old man. "Well, I'll try to keep it real simple … guess it's not that hard when you're as simple as me!" he laughed. "Anyway, as I was tellin' ya … we is supposed to be nothing but swirlin', vibratin' energy, accordin' to dis Einsteiny bloke. Den he says dat da slow-movin' energy is easy to see - like trees and rocks and carrots and tings - but our eyes aren't built for de faster energy and so we can't see it. Den I wondered if dese Zulus and Aborigines 'ad found a way to speed up deir energy so I couldn't see it. Hell, knowin' the little dat I know, it's the best answer I could come up with. What do you tink, laddie?

"I suppose you could be right, Sir. I really don't know," said the boy, trying hard to grasp everything the old man said. "But what has that got to do with the way we're built?" he asked.

"Aha, now comes da tricky bit!" the old man exclaimed, waving his finger in the air. "You see, this brainy Einsteiny bloke worked out that sound goes at a certain speed and light goes a little faster. Dat's why you see da lightnin' bafore you hear da tunder - da light gets to you before da sound does. You understand dat bit?"

"Yes, I think so," said the boy, starting to get really interested.

"Good. Dis took me a while but you're gettin' it real quick. Must be the schoolin' ya get," said the old man, pleased with the boy's interest. "Now look at me face and see dat me ears are lower than me eyes. I hope so, anyway!"

The boy nodded in agreement.

"Now, as you will know, you 'ave five senses,'" said the old man, patiently.

The boy looked puzzled.

"Well how do you know about anyting?" asked the old man.

The boy shrugged, totally confused.

"You know by feeling, tasting, smelling, hearing and seeing - your five senses," said the old man.

"Aah, yes!" said the boy, feeling a cloud of confusion lifting.

"And according to dis Einsteiny, our sense of touch (you know, hard physical tings) goes at a slower vibration than, say our sense of smell. So, it's easy! Da bits on your face, and yer arms, are in the same order as da vibration they connect with. Da higher da vibration, the higher up yer body the sensor is. I don't tink Einsteiny tought of dat one!", said the old man, looking pleased with himself.

The boy was stunned. It was all so simple!

"Now," said the old man, "what is dis ting dey call our sixth sense?"

"I .. I .. don't know," said the boy, feeling the confusion descend again.

"Simple!," said the old man, with a grin. "It's tought which comes in at da top of our heads."

"That's where thoughts come from?" asked the boy, thrilled to find the answer to an old question.

"Let's look at it nice and simple, like," suggested the old man. "Let's us say dat our sense of touch is a rock, the slowest and densest vibration. Then our taste is da root of a plant, like we taste carrots - it's more alive than a rock coz it grows, but stuck in da ground. So following on, our sense of smell is the flower of the plant, above da ground, waving around but can't move away. Are you following dis?"

"Yes, I think so," said the boy, quite enthralled.

"So, what would ye say be da sense of hearing," asked the old man.

The boy thought for a while and suddenly had a brain-wave. "It would be the animals because they move around and make noises!" he exclaimed.

"Excellent!" enthused the old man, rather enjoying this. "Excellent! All of the last ones are connected to the earth and are the ways we communicate with nature. So what about our sense of sight?"

The boy thought but couldn't think of the answer.

"What big bright thing allows you to see?" asked the old man, encouragingly.

"I don't know," said the boy, feeling a little dumb.

"The sun, of course!" said the old man, brightly. "Dat's how we connect to our solar system, trough the sun. And so our sixth sense, our "just knowin' tings" sort of sense connects us to the whole universe, where all knowing is. What is it, do you tink?"

"Don't know," said the boy, meekly.

"Yes you do, I just told you - "knowin' tings". It's tought and aint no different to sound or light, except it goes a little faster," said the old man, feeling quite pleased with himself. "Now don't ya tink it's funny dat we have five senses and also five fingers."

"But you said we had six senses," said the boy, confused again.

"My, you have been listening!" said the old man, impressed. "Let's leave the tought one out for a second coz most folks don't know 'bout dat one. Now, none of your fingers would be much use by demselves, now would dey?"

"I suppose not," said the boy, not knowing the relevance of hands and fingers.

"Well, so we have a palm dat connects and coordinates da fingers. So, what in your body, would be the central ting dat controls and coordinates the senses?"

"The heart," he said, without thinking, for it was the most central bit.

"Brilliant!" exclaimed the man. "Dis schooling does wonders for yer brains, don't it. So your heart is for your senses what your palm is for your fingers. Now, where does dis tinking sense come in to dis picture?"

"I'm not really sure," said the boy slowly, determined to find an answer, but unable to. "It's your arm!" he suddenly exclaimed, having the thought just before the old man spoke.

"Whew, you are good!" laughed the old man. "And your arm connects you to yer brain, which controls your whole body. What does your sixth sense, your tinking, connect you to?"

"Is it God?" asked the boy, meekly, fearing a wrong answer.

"Incredible," said the old man, wiping his brow. "And you have worked all dis out in less dan an hour and it took me sixty years! Wish I had gone to school - I might 'ave been like Einsteiny!"

"Do you mean that God controls us through the sun and we can just connect to him with thought," asked the boy, excited by his own revelations.

"As I said, I might have it all wrong so be careful of what I've said," said the old man.

"But it seems so simple, it must be right," said the boy, happily.

"Yes, yer right dere. The most right tings are da simplest ones," sighed the old man.

"Can I help you with your gardening, please," asked the boy.

"Sure," said the old man. They chatted and gardened until it was time to go home. The boy promised to stop by tomorrow as this learning was so much more fun than school was. Just as he was about to leave (with some potatoes for his mother) the old man stopped him.

"Oh, I forgot," he said. "The other really important reason for your eyes being above your mouth is dat you can look your girlfriend in the eye when you kiss her!"

"Ooh, yuck!" said the boy, running off and wondering if the face was such a good design after all.

Separating The Trees

After months of slothfulness and inactivity, hunched over a computer screen, it was time for exercise and health. Mr Health and Mr Aliveness were bursting to get out of this limp and flaccid body. So, a stretch of yoga and into the running shoes for a jog around the orchard.

It was so expansive exercising outside again, breathing in that fresh air, stretching the body and the lungs. I chatted to the trees, the grass, the kiwifruit, the earth and all around me. I was so thankful for their greenery, their beauty and the loving goodness they put into the soil and the air. The sparrows, fantails, pukekos, waxeyes, hens and rabbits all crossed my path and we exchanged pleasantries. The air was happy, the birds and animals were happy, the soil was happy and so was I. The recent rain had given everything a clean and sparkly look, and aliveness was all around.

My unfit body balked at the strain on it and puffed and sweated, but was joyful for the exercise and Mother Nature, until half-way round the circuit when I stopped, slamming into an invisible wall of despair. Before me there used to be a grove of oranges and mandarins - dark green and orange, giving colour and contrast to the duller green of the kiwifruit. That was no more. There was, now, nothing but grass, a few scattered fruit, a pile of ashes and mounds of dirt where the trees had been torn from the ground.

Stock still, I was devastated and then, once over the shock, began to cry. The crying turned to heart-wrenching sobs and I crouched on that rain-soaked ground and added my tears to those of the sky. I sobbed, loud and painfully, and prayed to the birds and the trees and anyone else who listened, "How do we stop this mindless slaughter, this wrench and burn mentality? Please! What can I do to look after Mother Earth, and to show others how to?" I was feeling desperate for my Mother and it was as if someone had attacked my own birth mother, and ripped at her skin without a care.

The sobbing, pleading and questioning continued for the longest time - I felt timeless, almost as if we had run out of it. Perhaps that was part of my desperation - was it getting too late to save Mother Earth and the rest of us? The desperation and despair racked my body uncontrollably and I cried to the trees, the sky, the soil, the birds - "Please help us help you. What can we do? How can we help? How can I get people to realise their oneness, their love for The Mother and all of her beings? That her devastation is our ruin and her abundance is ours?" An out-of-control little man against the whole world of uncaringness and separation - what could I do to change things? The despair led to more sobs and tears.

At some stage my logical brain started up (as yours probably has, Dear Reader) and began to wonder why an acre of uprooted citrus trees should have such a profound effect on me. Was I mad? Had the strain of work finally led to this mental break-down? No. I knew with absolute clarity that I was very sane and sensible. So, why the sudden and massive despair attack?

The size of the attack still surprises me but the reasons became clear through the continuing sobs and pleas for help. It was not the action taken by this orchardist, Syd, but the lack of thought and awareness behind it. I could feel the emptiness, the lifelessness in this acre of grass, dirt lumps, ashes and scattered fruit. The soil was sad, the tall shelter trees were sad, the birds and rabbits had all left and the space was sad and despairing of Man's separation from himself.

Syd is a good man, generous, good natured and humorous. A good man. He did not tear out those trees with anger, revenge or any other evil thought. The pity of it was that there was no thought at all - no thought for the trees as he contemplated and tore those standing ones from their homes. And that, I realized, was the problem.

Nature is just so willing to give its bounty for food, clothing, homes and health, but we take without gratitude. That saddens and weakens Nature. She gives unconditionally and unceasingly of her goodness and her love and we snatch and take without a thought of reverence or care for whence it came.

Those poor trees had grown and birthed their thousands of orange love-balls for us and the birds to eat. Millions of worms, nematodes, rhizobia and other creepy crawlies had nourished the soil for that growth, as had the sun, rain and countless other nature beings, unseen to us. That effort and love was with total cooperation from every team member, all working together in perfect harmony. If all had been paid at the going rate then each tree would have cost millions of dollars. In spite of this continuous, never-ending and massive effort, we are unable to see or appreciate it. We see a tree as a tree, separate from the soil that birthed it, separate from the sky that nourished it, separate from the beings that aerated and fed it, separate from ourselves. It is a thing without feelings or soul and can be chopped down or wrenched out with no thought of the effort or love that has gone in to create that beauty.

It seemed that Nature was quite happy to be moved around, torn out, chopped down and manipulated by Man, as long as it was done with love, with appreciation and gratitude for all that was, all that is. The sadness in this tiny space symbolized that of all Mother Earth, in that we separate ourselves from all other beings. I realized my sobbing and desperation was for all of our Mother, our whole Earth who is pleading with us to love her, become (once again) part of her, listen to her and appreciate her love and effort for us. For when we attack our Mother, we are attacking ourselves. When we put a wall of separation between us, that wall encloses us into a space of insensitivity, lack, fear and bitterness. We then fight and attack Nature and ourselves. The result is a very sick Mother and a bitter, fearful and divisive human race, fearing all that is different from him. When we see separation, it all becomes complex and very hard work - we find we have to battle all the way.

There are no boundaries in Nature. Every tree loves every other tree, every bird loves every other bird, plant and animal and that love sees them cooperating in the simplest and most powerful ways. Love is so simple. Its power overwhelms and the bounty that springs from it is so pure there can be nothing but growth and joy.

Knowing what can be, what will be, adds to my despair for that is so far removed from that which is. I cannot see across the ravine. The bridge to Oneness and Love seems so shaky, I wonder if humans will make it. I know we will, but I wonder how and when. The intuitive knowing is that we will walk that bridge, but the logical mind cannot span the ravine. As I analyse, I despair and as I intuit, I feel better, though still sad.

The trees have gone, torn and burned, but their seeds wait on the ground for us to plant and nourish. I wonder how long those seeds will have to wait. Perhaps they wonder that too, or do they know more than I?

Sunsets

In 1995 I spent a few days with a Maori kaumatua, an elder, and at one point, he said to me, "Philip, you've been to university and have done many things ... you're pretty intelligent aren't you?"

I nodded uncertainly, knowing that that I was in for one of his curly questions.

"Tell me then," he said with a sly smile, "tell me about the sun."

"What do you want to know about the sun?" I asked, knowing we were about to have the sort of discussion I had never had in a conventional school.

"Well, what I want to know from you is about sunsets ... what do your universities tell you about them?" he asked.

"Umm, I'm not sure," I said, "I studied accounting, economics and business and we didn't talk about sunsets ... what do you want to know about them?"

"Well, why do we have sunsets?" he asked.

"Because the earth is turning and if the sun is standing still, it must be behind the earth half of the time and so it looks like the sun is going round us but it's actually us that are going round and..." I started to explain in my logical way.

"Well, why does the sun change colour?" he asked.

"I don't really know," I said, suddenly stumped for an answer. I knew that he actually knew the answer but was, as often before, pretending not to know - this was part of knowledge-sharing game he often played.

"Well, I'll tell you," he said. "You see, when the sun first comes up, it is deep red. Then, as it rises further, it turns bright orange and then is yellow for the day until it turns orange and then deep red again as it disappears over the horizon. Tell me why that happens."

"I don't really know," I said, searching my mind for a simple scientific answer.

"They don't tell you about this at your universities?" he asked with a twinkle in his eye.

"No," I said, "they tell us how to count money, how to make more money, how to get jobs that give us more money and how to count all that extra money we were making but they didn't tell us why the sun changes colour at sunrise and sunset."

"Hmm, very useful information," he mused with a chuckle. "With all that money knowledge, you probably won't want to know about the colours of the sun, will you?"

"Of course I want to know and you know it!" I said, chuckling with him.

"Are you sure? It won't make you much money?" he said, smiling a little.

"Yes Koro, I'm very sure," I said, getting impatient.

"Does the sun hurry to know everything?" he asked, changing the subject annoyingly.

"Well, no," I said, feeling tension rising.

"And it's been around for a while?" he asked.

"Yes, forever," I said, wondering where this new conversation was going.

"Forever ... and it never hurries," he mused, stroking his chin. "And does it make much money?"

"No ... none at all ... what's the relevance of this?" I asked, feeling as if I was about to fall into yet another trap.

"Oh, no relevance at all," he said, with a smile. He then stood up slowly, grimacing and straightening his leg with obvious pain. "This damned arthritis - just lucky it's only in one knee ... so many other parts of me have been spared." I waited, knowing that the more I pushed to find the answer about the sunset, the more I'd have to wait for an answer. "I notice you've become a little more patient over these last three days," he said, nodding and smiling.

"The knowledge only comes when the questions stop," I said, repeating his words of three days ago.

                    51 Moments With Fables

"Pooh! And you don't even have a brown skin!" he said, bursting into laughter. He eased himself back down into his tattered armchair. "You're the whitest Maori I've ever met - you're actually listening ... it's a long time I've been waiting for you and I'm not really surprised. It's good to know my tupuna are right, as usual.

He often talked to and referred to his tupuna, his dead ancestors, and though I didn't totally understand how he could have been waiting for me, I knew I would find the answer by not asking the question - he seemed to know exactly what I knew and what I didn't and would actually tell me everything I needed to know. It was just very frustrating to know that I'd never know when the next gem of information would be shared with his unpredictable and illogical way of teaching.

"So, the sun," he said.

"Oh!" I exclaimed, being brought back unexpectedly to the original question.

"Yes, the sun," he said mysteriously, "it wants you to know its answer now."

"The sun does?" I asked, surprised.

"My tupuna say it is time for you to know," he said.

"I just don't know the answer," I said.

"The answer would be clear if you walked in thankfulness," he said, "because the reason the sun takes the trouble to turn itself red (before returning to its natural yellow) each morning and evening is that it is thanking its God for the day - the day that will be or the day that has been. Now how do you thank your God - with a word, smile, prayer or gesture of grateful thankfulness or do you do it with your morning and evening newspapers and television news programs that are mainly of tragedy, gossip and pain?"

My sheepish smile was all the answer he needed.

The Loss

Oh, handsome Jack,
Looked through a crack,
What did he see?
Pretty Marie.

Wearing no dress,
Hair a mess,
Britches are down,
Wearing a frown.

What does he think?
His face going pink,
Oh, what to do?
Mind in a stew.

Opens the door,
Expecting encore,
Shows his face,
With good grace.

"Oh, Marie dear,
I am here,
Saving you now,
This timely hour."

"Why don't you wear,
Knickers up here,
Satin and lace,
In the right place?"

Pretending to aid,
This pretty maid,
Hoping there'll be,
Opportunity.

"Oh, silly man,
I had no plan,
Happened all jumbled,
Now I've been rumbled."

"I'm not so fine,
Once it was mine,
Now it's lost, oh dear,
Just gone, disappear."

"I've looked under here,
And down there,
This thing I wore,
Don't have no more."

"A sweet young lad,
Now bounder and cad,
Came with his lyre,
Set me on fire."

"Got me all panting,
With his gallivanting,
Then things came up,
Filled my cup."

"Off he rushed,
'n I felt crushed,
Taken my asset,
Without even asket."

"I've looked high and low,
But it don't show,
This gift I had,
'n I feel sad."

"He must have took,
While me he shook,
My beautiful prize,
Pretty in my eyes."

"What do you call,
This gift that fall,
My name's Jack,
And I'll get it back."

"Thank you kind sir,
My heart does stir,
Your kind thoughts,
And helpful retorts."

"Not sure we'll find,
This thing was mine,
May not come back,
Stop smiling Jack!"

"Gone like mist,
When we kissed,
May not return,
Though I do yearn."

"This thing I had,
Now with sweet lad,
Is named, you see,
Virginity."

Birthdays and Moving On

We celebrated Anna's birthday today. Given that most people – older people anyway – don't like getting older, I'm bemused that any of us want to celebrate the only day in the year that we get older … more logical, I muse, to celebrate every other day of the year we don't get older.

Anna remarked, as she sipped her birthday champagne, munched her birthday chocolate and opened another birthday present, that this is the first birthday she's had, since 2003, that is in the same house as the previous year.

The last time I had a birthday in the same house as the year before was in 2000 … what wanderers we are! It must be time to move again … ah, I just remembered that we're moving up to Oxfordshire in 1½ weeks. Whew! Just had the scary thought of staying still for a moment and felt quite overcome with dread! I can relax again …

This was in 2011 and, since then, we moved to Oxford. After that, I moved to Australia and infested seven different houses till I ended up where I am now, in 2016. After Oxford, Anna moved to New Zealand and stayed in four different places before rejoining me in Australia. We have promised ourselves that we will stay here for at least another two years. Yeah, right!

The Pink Monkey

Let me tell you a story,
'Bout a monkey who felt he was borey..ng,
What would others think,
If I became pink?

He raced up a tree,
To see who he could see,
But they all looked and ran,
At this vision - a pink orangutan..g.

For pink's O.K.
At the end of the day,
On gorillas' tongues,
And baboons' bums.

But a monkey's brown,
And you don't mess around,
With paint that's loud,
Standing out in a crowd.

Coz pink made him happy,
And a clever, clever chappy,
But friends on the run,
Made him so glum.

Why must he choose,
'Tween friends he might lose,
And the joy he might gain,
From not being the same?

Pig In Tree

Sitting up a little tree,
Sat a little piggy-wee,
Looking pink, wide-eyed and shaky,
And far from her family.

"Well I never," said Miss Horse,
Looking up, with a smile, of course,
"What do I see through the gorse,
A pig on a spit, without any sauce?"

"I'm not for eating ," cried our porker,
Wondering who else would stalk her,
"Just joking," laughed our horse, a cheeky talker,
"But why are you up there, a climber, not a walker?"

"It's some story, short and very silly,"
Said our piggy friend, feeling like a dilly,
"So don't laugh at me, Miss Filly,
Or tell anyone else, will 'ee."

"I'll keep my face as straight as a pan,"
Said the horse, wondering if she can.
"Well, I had lots of breakfast," said Pig, "Lots and lots of bran,
Then diahorea set in and I ran and ran and ran."

"Oh dear," said Horse, suppressing a smile,
"Your bottom must have felt so sore and vile,
Letting go of that monstrous pile."
"Yes it did," said Piggy, liking a horse with style.

"Now," said Piggy, "came the strangest part.
After much plopping and then the odd fart,
I was so tired and sore in the heart,
My body did crash and wouldn't restart."

"Then I awoke, all up in the air,
And couldn't come down, without a stair,
And pigs don't fly and jumping I don't dare,
But staying up here just ain't fair."

"But," said Horse, "I still don't know,
Why it's up in a tree that you grow,
Pretending, maybe, to be a crow,
And not on the ground, you silly sow."

"Well, I'm guessing this bit - it might not be true,
But I slept and snored so long, after my poo,
Which fertilized a twig, which grew and grew,
And here I am looking down at you."

"So what's the moral, you with the trotter?
When you eat your bran, don't have a lotta,
Cause it makes your botter get hotter,
And up in a tree you're shotta?"

"No," said Piglet, with a tear in her eye,
"I'm lost from my sty,
Up in a tree, in the sky,
And all I want to do is cry."

"So proud of my doings,
I sat and wallowed in pride - better than others,
Now looking down on my kin,
Better and higher, but going nowhere."
"And I've lost my rhythm and rhyme."

Jimmy The Walrus

We teachers are supposed to supervise exams actively – constantly pacing up and down while looking stern and forbidding. However, I have trouble with pacing and stern. Besides, the students were all behaving perfectly under our sternness and forbiddingness and didn't seem to be cheating and, if they were, they were the ones who'd have to live with that cheatingness. So, there I was, supervising an exam in a rather ... um, shall we say, relaxed way ... and, while relaxing, my mind went wandering and my pen followed, which just goes to show that you can write anywhereyoubloomingwelllikeandatanytimeyoulike. Here's where my mind and pen went ...

In the land of bouncing camels and roaring turtles there lived a little boy and a little girl. There were a nice little boy and a nice little girl. In fact, they were so nice the flurtle tigers and whoobing wombats stayed away from them; they only liked not-nice people.

The little boy really wanted to be friends with the local policeman, a flying tiger, and the family of whooping wombats next door but they were having none of it. Every time Jimmy – yes, isn't that a nice little name for a nice little boy? – decided to be nice and pick up litter off the wombats' front lawn, they'd whoop out the back and either leap the fence and go on holiday or roll up and disguise themselves as fluffy hedgehogs. Or when Jimmy decided to be nice and tell the local policeman about the academic antelopes who were reading all night and keeping people awake with their lights on and page-turning sounds, the policeman would open his wings and fly to Switzerland and ski with Panda, the King of Cute – a place where everything was black and white and no other colour – till the snow melted or until Jimmy went off and pestered somebody else.

Jimmy was sure the wombats really didn't want to go on holiday every Thursday or that the nice policeman didn't want to go skiing with the King of Cute every Saturday afternoon, but he couldn't guess what made them rush off so suddenly and maybe he was wrong; maybe they did like going away unexpectedly, so regularly. But Jimmy wasn't sure. He had this sneaking suspicion it was something to do with him but he was too nice to say anything and that extra bit of niceness made the rest of his neighbours – even the slyly stoats who were so brave and stupid they didn't mind most nice people – try to get away to where the bouncing camels never went but wished they did.

Then, one nice sunny day when Jimmy was trying to be nice, his sister, Gemma (now, isn't that a nice name for a nice little girl?), who was just a little bit less-nice than Jimmy, detected some not-niceness coming off him. Jimmy was trying really hard to be nice but Gemma was not to be fooled – a nearly-not-so-nice person can detect nearly-not-niceness anywhere at any time for any reason anyhow. She asked Jimmy why he wasn't being totally nice (nearly-nice people can ask about nearly-niceness but nice people can't ... or won't) and he very nicely told her he was only being nice.

She quite-nicely told him she didn't believe him and he started to cry, which wasn't very nice for her to see. She had never seen this before as nice people don't cry but just always keep nice smiles on their faces. Now Jimmy's smile had fallen off and what had fallen on was a sad and grumpy face – not the face Gemma was used to seeing. She ran off to her parents who were actually whumping walruses, very cleverly disguised as people. You could tell this from the snorfelling noise they made when they slept but that's another story. Their names were Walruslea and Walruslen but everyone called them Lea and Len so their secret was safe. Anyway, back to Gemma – she ran to say Jimmy's face had fallen off and a not-nice one had grown out in its place.

They looked at each other, puzzled, Lea and Len did, and then they looked back at Gemma, all the while trying to hide their long tusks in their shirts. She said the same thing again so they were no wiser and so they sort of whumped out of the kitchen (looking back at the massive fish tank, longingly) and followed Gemma to where Jimmy and his new face were last seen.

Strangely, Jimmy was there but his new face wasn't – he'd somehow got his old nice face back and it was saying nice things. But Gemma didn't believe it as the smell of not-niceness still came off from some part of him.

A harping seagull went flying past and said, "Pooh! Smells like a not-nice rubbish dump!" And he flew on shaking his beak as if there was nose pooh stuck to it. A mooching mole heartily agreed and went away, mooching through the ground at twice the speed.

Jimmy was bothered by all this and he started to feel not-nice and so he was bothered twice over and he said a not-nice word: "Bother!"

"Jimmy!" said Lea, "That's not nice."

"Sorry, mamawal, but I'm trying really, really hard to be nice but not-nice keeps coming into my head."

"Your head?"

"My head."

"Just your head?"

"Well, it's slipping down into my tummy, too," said Jimmy, trying to be nice about explaining not-nice.

"Oh!" said Len, looking seriously serious. "It's serious then."

"It's serious?" asked Gemma, looking alarmed and hoping it was a false alarm.

"If it stays in your head you can change-your-mind it out," explained Len, his big flipper tapping the floor. "But if it goes down into your tummy, you've got to deal with it."

"Deal with it?" asked Jimmy as the not-nice thing in his tummy got not-nicer. Really, really uncomfortable, really. "What's 'deal with it' mean, dadawal?"

"It sounds easy but it isn't, really," said Len, saying his words really slowly as if he was thinking really hard about each one before it came out of his mouth.

"Tell us what you're thinking," said papawal.

"Or feeling," said mamawal.

I can't," said Jimmy, screwing up his eyes as if he was about to cry. "It feels sort of, well, bad."

"And if you keep it in it will only get badder," said papawal.

"And then it will be too big for your mind to hold in and will explode," said mamawal, helpfully, as an exploding parrot popped in mid-air flight and crashed on the lawn.

"What?" asked Emma, her eyes nearly popping out of her face. "He'll explode?" Jimmy took a step back and teetered on the edge of the porch steps, nearly falling down them.

"No, not him, not Jimmy," said papawal, waving his left flipper with agitation. Then he realised it smelled badly of fish and tried to put it in his pocket, found it didn't fit and so put it behind his back like Prince Charles, whoever he is. "No, Jimmy won't explode …"

"The badness inside will explode," explained mamawal, interrupting her husband, helpfully … except that he didn't seem to look like she was helpful but she kept talking, helpfully: "You see, nothing ever stops, change is ever constant and that's the way."

Jimmy and Emma looked at each other, looked a bit confused, looked at their mother and looked more confused as their educated cat paraded by saying, in his odd Catalonian accent, "Everything gets bigger, it'll soon be a trigger so go figure." People and walruses looked confused while the cat looked clever and strutted off as he adroitly adjusted his sunglasses.

The stultifying, sultry silence that sauntered in gave papawal a perfect opportunity to say some more. He took the opportunity by the horns and said something: "What we're saying, children, is that whatever we focus on, gets bigger."

"What about diets and people who focus on losing weight?" asked Emma.

"Huh?" grunted papawal, looking like he'd been caught out stealing mackerels.

"Well, if people focus on losing weight, the losing weight will grow and there'll be more less weight," said mamawal. "Simple!"

Jimmy and Emma didn't look any less confused than they did a few moments before.

"So, whatever's in your head, Jimmy, will grow," said papawal before anyone else had a chance to look surprised or before another parrot could explode in the near vicinity. Or the far one as well. "If there's good thoughts in there, they'll grow and will explode in happiness thoughts and constructive deeds."

"And if you have bad thoughts in there, they'll keep growing till they're bigger than your brain and they'll have to burst out in bad feelings and destructive deeds," said mamawal butting in again, helpfully, while papawal scowled just a little bit.

"So how do I stop them?" asked Jimmy looking like a roaring turtle was about to bite him.

"Pop!" went another exploding parrot as a tangle of feathers pflumped to the ground.

"You can't," said mamawal and papawal, together in perfect harmony. They looked at each other and smiled crookedly as if something nice and unexpected had happened. I probably had.

"But I must be bad if I've got bad inside me," exclaimed Jimmy. "And I want to be nice." He sniffed a bit.

"Everyone has bad inside them, Jimmy. Absolutely everyone," said mamawal. "We all feel guilt, shame, sadness, anger and regret. Every one of us."

"But, but …"

"No but, Jimmy," said mamawal, holding up her flipper and smiling. "Everyone has bad thoughts about themselves, about other people and about things that happen. All of us have bad thoughts …"

"But what about all the nice people?" asked Jimmy, unable to stop himself interrupting.

"Everyone sad, everyone glad, no one bad, that's too bad," said the educated Catalonian cat as it strutted by, proudly showing off his new tartan jandals .

"There are no nice people, Jimmy," said papawal, quietly. "There are no right people or wrong people or nice people or not-nice people …"

"But, but …"

"But you were trying to be nice and I'm telling you no one can be nice, huh?"

"Uh, yes, I suppose so."

"Everybody's just people, just good people with bad stuff inside them," said papawal, leaning back against the veranda railing. He heard it crack as it wobbled a bit and so he stood up quickly, looking like he'd stolen another mackerel.

Jimmy and Emma giggled a bit and mamawal put a flipper over her mouth to stifle a smirk as papawal shuffled awkwardly on his back flippers.

"Excuse me sir, madam, your breakfast is served," said the pernicious penguin, appearing at the door and bowing slightly.

"Ooh, yum, fish porridge and tuna tea!" exclaimed papawal, apparently happy to have his embarrassment forgotten. "Bring it out here, Portly. We can eat it out here on the veranda today."

"As you wish, sir," said the penguin who disappeared so quickly that Jimmy wondered if he had ever been there. Then, before he took another breath – or so it seemed – the table cloth was laid and the table was set for four for breakfast, all shining silver and delicate crockery. As they sat down to a delishy fishy brekky, Jimmy kept thinking, Here I am with all these nasty thoughts and badness screaming around inside me and it's just the worst thing to ever happen and I'm the baddest boy around and they must hate me as I'm not nice and they should be ashamed and telling me I'm bad, naughty and not nice and … well, here they are, thinking about breakfast and their blubbery tummies when they should be angry and sad and disappointed that their nice little boy is not nice any more … and on and on his thoughts raged but, of course, he was too nice to say anything. Then Emma smiled at him the way sisters do when they realise they like their brothers and tears tried really hard to burst out of his eyes and he held them back so nobody would notice.

"Are you alright, Jimmy?" asked mamawal, sadly, as she tucked her napkin into her pyjama top and sprinkled seaweed salt on her porridge.

"Yes I'm fine, mamawal, really nice," said Jimmy, sweetly, as he thought, How did she know something was wrong when I hid it so well?

They ate in silence, as they often did, for the first few delicious mouthfuls as tigers flew overhead and camels bounced along the dirt road, kicking up puffs of dust that glinted in the sunshine.

This would be a perfect day in Quaradise, thought Jimmy, if I wasn't such a bad boy. But he hid the thought inside his brain so nobody could see it.

"Well, another perfect day in Quaradise!" said papawal, looking around blissfully with a large toothy and tusky smile on his whiskery face. Jimmy felt his heart stop and his face go hot as he dropped his spoon with a clang. "Yes, it's just marred a bit by Jimmy thinking he's bad when he's not." Papawal winked at Jimmy and Jimmy looked down and tried to stop his hands from shaking.

Oh, jolly giraffes, thought Jimmy, he can see my thoughts! Then a bigger, uglier thought flew through his brain. Eek, he's always known what I've been thinking! Oh, guzzling giraffes, every not-nice thought I ever thought he knows about. He must hate me … but he seems to like me and he's really kind and helpful to me. It felt like his face was going white or red or some other colour but he couldn't see as his eyes were looking the wrong way.

"Yes, my son, we do like you," said papawal, his flipper softly on Jimmy's hand. "People like you but they don't like your secrets and the fact that, one day, you're going to explode from them. They're just keeping themselves safe from your explosion."

Someone grabbed Jimmy's hand – well, that's what it felt like – and smashed it down into the porridge, spraying bits of fishy porridge and plate everywhere. "I don't keep secrets!" he yelled at everyone, all at once. "And stop getting at me and telling me what I think and what I should do and I'm not bad and I'm good and I don't believe you and I hate you all …" Then the words stopped and his brain stopped and his thoughts stopped and he felt soooooooooo ashamed of the outburst that his mouth yelled without asking him. It was as if he wasn't in control. But he was, really.

The penguin appeared at his side and he shouldn't have been surprised – it happened all the time – but he was when the mess of his breakfast suddenly wasn't there. Just gone. Mr Penguin was the perfect servant but it was still hard to believe how clever he was. Jimmy expected everyone else to disappear – or wished he could – but they were still there, smiling sweetly at him. He tried to stop it but his stupid face started crying and, in a whoosh!, Mr Penguin was back with a box of tissues and he was surprised and shouldn't have been.

Jimmy tried to calm himself down but the harder he tried, the more agitated he became. He clenched his fists and clenched his eyes and tried really hard to hold the agitation in but it just fought back and got bigger inside him. So he clenched harder and clenched his bottom and clenched his knees as well but the agitation grew even more. It grew so big, in fact, that it threatened to overwhelm him and then the terror of being taken over and out of control grew up and joined in the grim dance of madness as he realised he was losing control and so tried to clench everything twice as much as before.

As he did this, the Catalonian cat tip-toed past, muttering, "Holding

51 Moments With Fables

it in is no sin but makes a din and you tumble in." The cat looked so silly – especially with the bowler hat and the clown nose – that Jimmy started to giggle. He clenched his mouth to stop himself laughing but when the cat did a pirouette and showed off his bunny tale, Jimmy knew he couldn't keep the giggle in. The giggle grew into a silly laugh and then into a belly laugh and, soon, he was doubled over laughing and crying. The cat winked, waved his umbrella and slipped out the door as Jimmy fell to the floor clutching his sore tummy, unable to stop shaking and laughing. But he did stop, eventually, and he lay there exhausted, panting and sweetly empty.

Then, with a shock, he sat up and realised the anxiety and terror had left him. He looked around as if he might find them (the anxiety and terror) skulking in some corner and then shook his head, wondering where they had gone and, more confusing, how he had got them to go. He shook his head again and the beginning of an answer came to him. Perhaps, just perhaps, they'd gone when he'd lost control, when laughter overtook him and he could think of nothing but silliness, happiness and a sore tummy. It didn't really make sense but maybe, just maybe, it was giving up control. Or maybe it was focusing on something else – something deliriously, insanely happy – that made them go.

Then a strange thing happened. Well, it was a strange thing for Jimmy. A passing tiger flew past, suddenly stopped and plumped himself on Jimmy's lawn. There was a puff of dust, a scampering of thwirtle mice and, from the tiger, a strange sound that is probably spelt like urrmmthwop. It is possible the tiger didn't mean the ground to be so close or for himself to be going so fast and that inopportune point for his eyes seemed to spin like twirling bats and his jaw shook like a dancing elephant. It's also possible that twenty worms and six centipedes had heart attacks, underground, but Jimmy has yet to hear from them.

The tiger flumped onto his back with his wings outstretched in the grass and his legs straight up in the air. Jimmy thought he was dead (the tiger, not Jimmy who knew he wasn't dead because he was thinking about the possibility of a tiger being dead and dead people don't think … well, he didn't think they did) till he noticed the tiger's tummy quivering and his eyes still spinning. Jimmy wasn't used to dead tigers but he guessed this wasn't one of them. He hoped so, anyway.

Now, it's a funny thing about tigers that they can either be really grumpy, growly and eat you or they can be really purry, smiley and can hug you. Jimmy liked hugs but not being eaten and quickly realised that being eaten meant he wouldn't be hugged ever again. So he backed away from the edge of the verandah.

"Jimmy, Jimmy," said papawal with a fatherly flipper on Jimmy's shoulder. "There's no need to run. He's our friendly policeman. He won't hurt you."

The tiger rolled over, picked up his head, put it back on and looked back to see his tail was missing.

"It's over there, in the hedge," yelled papawal from the verandah.

"Uh, thanks Wal," said the tiger, looking a trifle embarrassed as he turned a yellowy shade of red. "The silly thing just won't stay stuck."

"Oh my golly wobbles," said papawal, stroking his chin and frowning, his eyebrows wobbling gently. "I wouldn't have thought a tail could fall off."

"I know," said the tiger, retrieving his tail from the hedge, dusting it off and clicking it back on to his bum. "That's all I ever think about now; my silly tail falling off."

"Why don't you stop thinking about it?" asked Jimmy, wondering where his words came from. Then more turned up in his mouth and made him say them. "If you think about something all the time, it will happen all the time."

"Really?" asked papawal.

"Really?" asked the tiger.

"Uh, gosh, I think so. The words told me to say them so I did. They're usually right," said Jimmy, stroking his chin and frowning, his eyebrows not wobbling. He suddenly felt quite nice inside and everyone smiled.

Then I leapt into next week as someone bellowed, "Time's up, everyone. Put your pens down and we'll collect your papers!" With great presence of mind, I leapt up (did I already say that?) and mimed those words along with the other teacher so they'd think I said it and not suspect that I'd been supervising the exams ... um, shall we say, relaxed way ... and not writing this amazing story. Which just goes to show you can write anywhereyoubloomingwelllikeandatanytimeyoulike.

                    51 Moments With Fables

Believing In Science?

Many years ago science - based on the need to prove that God lived on Earth - proved that everything went round the earth. It was only when Galileo questioned the whole rationale, that it was discovered that science was wrong.

For many years, scientists proved that it was impossible for a human being to run a mile in under four minutes. Then, in 1954, Roger Bannister ran the mile in 3 minutes and 59.4 seconds. In the last 50 years the mile record has been lowered by almost 17 seconds.

Science is currently proving that our naughty emissions are causing global warming and all sorts of terrible climate change effects. At the same time, Mars has developed two rivers (that were never there before) and is undergoing massive climate change. I guess we either:

1. Need to tell the Martians to stop using aerosol sprays and burning petrol, or

2. Realise that it's not all about us (as Galileo suggested) and that there are forces far greater than us controlling things.

I'm just waiting for science to prove that science doesn't exist and they got it all wrong … most of the time. I could be waiting for a long time, though!

Economic Recovery

It is the month of August, on the shores of the Black Sea. It is raining and the little town looks totally deserted. It is tough times, everybody is in debt and everybody lives on credit. Suddenly, a rich tourist comes to town.

He enters the only hotel, lays a 100 Euro note on the reception counter, and goes to inspect the rooms upstairs in order to pick one.

The hotel proprietor takes the 100 Euro note and runs to pay his debt to the butcher.

The butcher takes the 100 Euro note, and runs to pay his debt to the rancher.

The rancher takes the 100 Euro note, and runs to pay his debt to the supplier of his feed and fuel.

The supplier of feed and fuel takes the 100 Euro note and runs to pay his debt to the town's prostitute who, in these hard times, gave her "services" on credit.

The hooker runs to the hotel, and pays off her debt with the 100 Euro note to the hotel proprietor to pay for the rooms that she rented when she brought her clients there.

The hotel proprietor then lays the 100 Euro note back on the counter so that the rich tourist will not suspect anything.

At that moment, the rich tourist comes down after inspecting the rooms and takes his 100 Euro note, after saying that he did not like any of the rooms, and leaves town.

No one earned anything. However, the whole town is now without debt, and looks to the future with unbounded optimism.

Thank you

I am able to put these intangible ideas into words and Anna, my wife, is able to put them into action; the reason she's such a good life coach. She is my best friend and greatest inspiration and I thank her from the bottom of my beating heart for being there, for loving me and for being that which I wish for myself.

Anna edited this book with her razor eye for the details I didn't see. Thank you for seeing that which I cannot ... on so many levels.

Emily Cooney, who I accidentally met at the Brisbane Writers Festival, took on the challenge of turning 10 of my books into e-books. Thank you for your internet and tech saviness ... and for your enthusiasm.

And to Yangrui Gao, a Chinese student of mine who loved a good joke, hard work and to draw pictures of me on the white board for my surprised arrival. You made my day sweet, so many times, Yangrui. And it's one of your drawings on the front cover, my friend.

I am also indebted to *A Course in Miracles* - and all the people I have met through it - for it shows me the way to peace; that way that is both simple and difficult. Forgiveness is simple but it's difficult to do in every second of our lives.

I keep trying ...

If you enjoyed this book enough to buy one for a friend - or yourself, your best friend - just wave your smart phone over this Quick Response (QR) Code and you'll be taken to my website at www.philipjbradbury.com

Or, if you want to check out - or buy - the next book in the series, *43 Moments With Men*, use this QR Code.

About the Author

In New Zealand I experienced life as an accountant, credit manager, company director, shepherd, scrub-cutter, tree pruner, freezing worker, plastics factory worker, saxophonist, army driver, tour bus driver, stage and television actor and singer, builder, lecturer, facilitator for men's groups, reporter, columnist, magazine editor, publisher, writer ...

In South Africa as an AIDS workshop co-facilitator ...

In the Australian bush as a barman, horse and camel trekker and stock-whip teacher ...

In England as a contract accountant, corporate trainer, estate manager, lecturer, singer/songwriter, website editor/writer and freelance writer …

Now that I'm back in Australia, house renovating, teaching and writing, I'm wondering what's next!

The constant for my wife and I is *A Course in Miracles*, a psychological life-style course in forgiveness. Through it I have found the peace I had always been searching for - the journey to where we have always been.

Philip J Bradbury in social media
About Me: https://about.me/philipbradbury
Amazon: amzn.to/25X0CLb
Facebook:
   https://www.facebook.com/AuthorPhilipJBradbury/
Google+: http://bit.ly/2bsbpUy
Linked In - http://bit.ly/2aTzZMS
Pininterest: https://au.pinterest.com/bradburywords/
Smashwords: http://bit.ly/2aNjkic
Twitter: https://twitter.com/PhilipJBradbury
Website: www.philipjbradbury.com
Wordpress blogs:
   https://flashfictionfanatic.wordpress.com/
   https://pjbradbury.wordpress.com/

                                   51 Moments With Fables

53 Moments
With
Fables

Philip J Bradbury

Published by   The Write Site,
Brisbane, Australia

Other books by Philip J Bradbury

Non-Fiction
Whose Life Is It Anyway?
The Lawless Way
Change Your Mind, Change Your World
The Twelve Week Miracle (with Anna Bradbury)
Understanding Men
Articles of Faith
Conversations on Your Business
Stepping Out Of Debt and Into Financial Freedom

Some-Fiction
Dactionary – the dictionary with attitude
The Meaning of Larf
53 SMILES
97 SMILES
45 Moments With Men

Fiction
An Olympic Challenge
The Royal Bank of Stories
Circles of Gold
Gerald the Great of Gorokoland

Words in progress - looking for a publisher
40 Moments With Writing
55 Moments With God
65 Moments With Self
22 Moments With Odes
The Last Stand-Down
The Last Accusation
The Last Expulsion

For more information on these books, see
   www.philipjbradbury.com

www.ingramcontent.com/pod-product-compliance
Lightning Source LLC
Chambersburg PA
CBHW070305120726
47910CB00007B/2379